# Your Pal Andy

# By Thomas Clark

For Simon

# Table of Contents

# The Big Time

July 8th

Well Joe it has been a world wind few days and I have been showed round more stadiums than you have probily even been to but finely a club has made me an offer I coudent refuse and I have signed on the dotty line. It has been a big decision for me Joe as I do not believe in chopping and changing and I am not saying anything against you old pal as I guess you were only trying find a club where the manager woud give you a game from time to time but that is never going to be a problem for me and when I left the managers office today it was funny to think I am going to be here for the next 10 - 15 years and maybe longer if I get my coaching badges. But I am not wanting to get too far ahead of my self just yet Joe as I have to focus on the task at hand and that is the busness of helping this football club get back where it belongs.

I guess you know how hard it was for me to leave Selkirk Football Club Joe especially when the chareman still owes me that £100 pounds and if I am being honest it left kind of a sower taste in my mouth that nobody menshuned it to him and I woud have done it myself only old Hughies funeral did not seem like the right time. I hoped you or 1 of the other lads might have said something as it woud have been diffrent comeing from you but I guess I shoud not worry about a measeley £100 when I am going to be raking it in before long. It woud be cutting off my nose to spite my face to stay at Selkirk for the sake of £100 and in a year or 2 it will not be worth my time to pick up £100 if I drop it running for the bus. Not that I will be catching no busses when I am rich Joe but I dont know what else I woud be running for only I supose it is not realy the money that is the point Joe but the principal and if you coud menshun it to the chareman I would appresiate it as even tho I will be bringing down the big $ in a year or 2 right now it is all tied up in insentives eg I get payed whenever I score a goal which is money in the bank as they say Joe but not until I am playing games. Ever sints we booked Miyorka you have been like a broken record abt that money I owe you but if you reely needed it Joe you woud ask the chareman for my £100 and then we would be evens and it would killing 2 birds with 1 stone.

Anyway Joe when I left you said it woud be good if I dropped you a text every once in a wile but I thought you woud prefer a proper email as their is quite a bit to tell you abt and a text woud not do it all justice. When we booked it in Jan I bet you did not think you woud be off to Miyorka with a professhunal footballer come summer Joe altho it did not take no Misstic Meg to work out I woud not be plying my trade at Selkirk FC a hole lot longer. I supose it will be sort of a blow to my new manager to here I will be away during preseason but they will only be playing friendlys Joe and if anything it will help lower expectashuns a bit if they get beat a couple of times wile I am gone. The club must have left off asking for friendlys until the last minute at that as the teams we are up against are no grate sheiks Joe and what is the point of beating them when they are not even in the same league as you ie people will sit up and pay attenshun if you beat Barcalona but if you beat Notts County they woud not be able to make head nor tail of it and they woud just be wondring why you were even playing them the same as if you had played against a team of 10 yr olds and I am not saying anything against you Joe as I know they were your little cousins but most people woud think it was a bit strange is all I am saying.

Anyway Joe you can guess how over the moon the club are to have snapped me up and old Donaldson coud hardly keep the grin off his face when he walked past. I am the kind of person that sees things through Joe and they will get many years of good service out of me and you know better than anyone Joe that I am not the sort of person that will treat people diffrently even if I am a bit more important than them and if it turns out that I am too good for the club I will make sure they get a fare deal when they sell me on altho I guess if I win a trophy or 2 they will have come out prity well ahead and they coud not realy say anything if I moved on to better things. Because if they wanted to hang on to me Joe they might have gived me a contract for more than just a year tho of course I woudent have signed for more than 1 year on this money as at this rate I woud be better off getting a job at Tesco and mailing the club a check for a couple £100 pounds every month. But that is water under the bridge Joe and if I leave next summer you can at lease be sure that the chareman will not stiff me out of a measeley £100 just to prove a point about only going up for 1 serving at the kitchen and if he thinks those sausage rolls were worth £100 pounds I supose he must take out a second morgage every time he goes to KFC.

I have not met my team mates yet Joe as they are all away on holiday but you woud have to hate yourself prity bad to think you coud not get into this team ahead of them. A bit of leadership is realy what they need in midfeild rite now and somebody who can get the fans up out there seats altho as I say Joe I am focusing on the task at hand and that is to get this club back to where they belong and the rest can take care of itself as they say.

Anyway Joe that is all from me for now. I will drop you a line whenever I get the chance but I guess it will not be that often now I am in the big leagues.

Your pal,

Andy

July 9th



Well Joe I know I only emailed you yesterday and you have not had no chance to reply and even if you did what coud you say exept maybe the postman came at 10:10 today instead of 10:15 so you shoudent worry about writeing back as their is not realy much for you to say and I guess talking to me abt what you are up to rite now woud be the same as someone writeing to martin luthor king about there summer holidays altho I guess even martin luthor king never played in the premier league. I am not saying he did not acheive anything worthwhile Joe just that we all have our own tallents altho I supose that is not true of everybody and some people you wonder how they get there shoes tied in the morning without hanging there selfs. But what I am trying to say is Joe I hope you wont think I am turning into a big head just because I am doing something with my life and you do not need to let me know what you are up to exept maybe once in a wile as I can probily guess prity good. I have always treated you like we were equals Joe and there is no chance of that changeing just because I am going places and no matter how much I acheive or how much money I earn to me you will always be the same old Joe.

The club has found me a nice b&b and I am all settled in until I find a place of my own only I am not sure I will bother Joe as the weekly rate here is peanuts and there is a kettle and a sink and I am on the same floor with the bathroom plus somebody comes in to tidy my room every am so it seems like I am on to a prity good thing. The TV has only got 1 chanel but it turns out it is Eurosport so I stayed up til 3am last nite eating mars bars and watching the sumo wrestling.

You know Joe I woud never say anything against my fellow professhunal athletes but these sumo wrestlers got it so easy they make goalkeepers look like captains of industry. The matches only last about ½ minute a peace and there is no stratergy at all that I can tell. I have always said that it is good for sports people to have a bit of weight behind them no matter what old Blaikie used to tell us but I dont see why these sumo wrestlers have got to be so fat when if they was a little thinner they coud just turn the tables by jumping out of the way and the other guy would be flat on his face like that time you tried to rugby tackle Cammy McLeod in PE. But you know me Joe I have always been someone that likes to think with his brane and be 1 step ahead and I guess that is why I am sitting here in my own room with my own kettle instead of turning the laundery basket upside down looking for a pair of socks that smell ok. But the old sayings are true Joe when you pay peanuts you get monkeys and if you want to attract real tallent you have to be willing to pay the big $ and in that regard I guess sumo wrestling will all ways be stuck in the past.

Our 1st training session is a week on Monday Joe and I have been looking after my self quite well so I shoud think that I will pass with flying colours as they say and old Donaldson and the guys who have actually played some football will know that training is all abt seeing who has got the most ability on the ball and not just who can run the most laps or touch there own toes. I am not someone that likes to run there mouth off Joe as I have all ways done my talking on the pitch but there will be a lot of players on Mon whose mouths will be watering at the prospect of playing beside me this season and I dont think it will be long before people see that I am the missing piece of the puzzle altho from what I seen last season there puzzle has more pieces missing than a charity shop kitchen set.

I guess you will not have had the chance to see the chareman abt that £100 Joe but just thought I shoud remind you abt it anyway altho you do not normally need to be reminded when it comes to a pound or 2.

Your pal,

Andy

July 12th

Well Joe we have been called in to training early and the reason is that the club has won the UEFA fare play award and we have qualified for Europe. Our 1st game will be at the end of July so there is a lot to be done between now and then to jell the team together tho of coarse that will be a cinch for me Joe sints one of the big strenths of my game has always been knowing what other people are going to do before they even do it. People always say that I am good at reading the game and that is true Joe but I think it realy comes down to the fact that I am a prity good judge of character so I can always tell the mistakes people are going to make tho I guess I have had plenty of practise playing for Selkirk for 2 years. But it is quite unusual for a player like me to be able to tune in to team mates who are on a lower band width so to speak and you just have to look at how good a partnership I built up with you last season Joe even tho asking me to play anchor in that midfeild was a bit like making Einstine a milk monitor. It is good to be able to get inside the minds of player less talented than your self Joe but there is a natral limit to everything and there were times last year when it felt like the club must be making more money threw youtube fail videos than via cash at the gate tho of coarse I know you all ways tried your best Joe and at the end of the day it is the manager who picks the team not you.

But that is all in the past now Joe and I only mention it to show how much things have changed. It is hard to believe that in a couple of months I have went from drying myself with paper towels to playing in Europe agenst the crem della crem and it is a big shop window for me to tout my wears in as they say and I have all ways thought I woud adapped well to life in a diffrent country. When you watch Spanish football now a days you see loads of midfeilders like me in Spain and in Italy altho I woud draw the line at Germany Joe as it is just a free for all there and I like my legs fine where they are. But we probily wont get a team from Spain or Italy to begin with as in the 1st rounds it is all the little countrys that get a shot at it and that is the down side to wining the fare play award Joe as you wind up playing against teams of PE teachers and shoe salesmen and I guess if I had been here last season the club woud have qualified fare and square instead of by not tackling anyone from November on but that is in the past now Joe and my job is to get the club back to where it belongs and that starts by getting us through the 1st rounds in Europe. I guess there will be nobody at the club who has my level of experience when it comes to diddy teams only it will be a step up for me at that to be playing against postmen and dentists when most of the players at Gala Fairydean coud not hold down a job at bm bargens.

Your pal,

Andy


July 13th


Well Joe whenever you see all these TV programs or read comments on the internet abt how footballers get treated like roylety you can tell them from me that there is nothing in it and even playing for 1 of the biggest clubs in the country does not stop you from being treated like a 4 yr old or worse and I guess you can call off the trip to Miyorka Joe as our so called manager Mr Barry Donaldson does not think he can do without me for even 1 week when our only game is against a bunch of specky 12 year olds from Timbucktoo. It does not say much for his faith in the team Joe and if I was them

I woud be furious as realy he is saying they are not up to it which is probily true but it is not good for team moral from him to say like that.

What happened Joe was after training I went up to old Donaldsons office and asked him for a minute and he looked up at me and he said well either you are here to shake my hand and thank me for the opperunity or you are looking for some dieting tips because you cant have any problems after 1 day and I told him about the holliday to Miyorka and how long we had been planning it for and I even told him about how Tina broke up with you by text and how depressed you had been but it did not cut any ice with him at all Joe and he just sat there stoney faced and said well that is quite a storey all right and it woud be enough to bring a teer to a glass eye only you see I cant let you go to Spain when the whole of Europe is hoaching with spies that wants to find out our game plan and it woud be crazy to show them our hand this early on. But you are right and I can see just from looking at you that you need a holliday so what I will do is I will send you to Dunoon with our reserves next weekend and then you will have plenty of time to relax on the water front and have an ice cream or 3 and maybe even play a little football if the mood takes you.

Well of coarse Joe that is not what I had in mind and I dont know who our reserves are but on the bases of what I saw at training today picking out the worst XI would be like looking for hay in a haystack and when I told Donaldson that he dident seem to understand and he just kept saying it was the lease he coud do for me when I had obviously worked so hard to keep in shape during the off season and he had been worried sick in the canteen at lunchtime that I was going to burn my self out.

So Joe it looks like that is that and I wont be going to no Miyorka any time soon and you cant say I dident try and I even asked Brady the club captain if he could put in a word for me but he just laughed and said you couldent change old Donaldsons mind with a tire iron so I guess that means he wont be able to do it and I wont have any option but to give up on it. So I woud appresiate it if you coud go down to the travel agents Joe and explane to Alan what has happened and get me my money back and to be honest with you Joe I coud probily do with the money more than the holliday right now so I guess it is something of a blessing in disguise as they say.

Anyway Joe I think you will probily enjoy Miyorka a lot more if you go on your own as it must be hard all ways to be liveing in someone elses shadow and it is abt time some nice girl who is not hung up on looks and money gave you a 2nd glance because if character was what won football games Joe you woud be champion of the world only it isent of coarse and the cream will all ways rise to the top and I never yet heard of Barcalona signing someone on acct of his personality. But the point is Joe a clean brake is really what you need and to leave the past behind you and going to Miyorka woud be a chance to do that and if you coud remember to get the £500 pounds back from Alan that I already payed + the £100 pounds from the chareman and paypal them to me as soon as you coud Joe that woud be great.

Your pal,

Andy

July 14th


Well Joe I am sorry you feel that way about it and that you took it the wrong way and I thought you woud be glad of the chance to be your own man and step out of the shadows once in a wile as most people woud not be happy playing 2nd fiddle all there days but each to there own I guess and personly I would love to go on holliday by my self and not need to plan around somebody but as I say Joe not everyone has got big plans for themselfs and some people are happy just to do what they are told and it is nobodys busness to judge them even if it does look a bit funny to everyone else.

I am sure you did your best Joe but I realy wish you had been able to get my money back from Alan and he might have said at the time that it was non refundable but obviously when I was booking the holliday I was not planing to cancel it and it woud be a bit funny if someone was booking a holliday and they were already thinking abt not going so it woud not have registered with me even if he says he did say it. I only wish you had maybe tried a little bit harder with him Joe and I am not saying that you did not do your best but maybe if you had come at it from a diffrent angle the result woud have been diffrent and if you coud try him again Joe I woud realy appresiate it and I remember how much you used to perseveer when we were playing for Selkirk Joe and even when you were getting totally rinsed you woud stick on in their and we all ways used to say what a plucky little fellow you were and if you can keep on at Alan the same way you used to keep on at Eyemouth I am sure that you will get somewhere as where there is a will there is a way.

Tho of coarse Joe if you realy dident want to go on holliday by your self you could always give my place to someone else and I woud only ask back what I paid for it. Normally when you try to book a last minute holliday you wind up paying threw the nose but if you managed to find someone else who doesent mind going on holliday with you I woud only want my £600 pounds back and we woud say no more about it. I know you used to have that friend at collage who was into board games only you havent realy menshuned him in a wile so I dont know if you are still friends but maybe you coud ask him if he wanted to go as I am sure he woud.

Of coarse I had not forgotten about Tracy Joe and when I said all that about a nice girl finely taking a second look at you I just meant someone who doesent work in the same dept as you at Tesco and I woud never say anything against any girl who took a friendly intrest in my old pal Joe and it is out of order for you to say that I never realy liked her when I can hardly even remember who she is. If I had knowed you felt like that Joe I woud have offered to give up my space on the holliday long before now and if Tracy is interested in going to Miyorka with you then I would not charge her any more than any other friend of yours.

Anyway Joe let me know what you come up with as if you coud find somebody else to go with you or you coud find a way to get my money back from the travel agents it woud realy be killing 2 birds with 1 stone as they say.

Your pal,

Andy

July 17th

Well Joe I am sorry to here you are calling off Miyorka as I know how much you were looking forward to it but I am glad that at lease you were able to get ½ our money back altho I think you maybe coud have done better old pal if you had just come at it from a diffrent angle but a ½ is better than nothing as they say and the money will realy come in handy as the club have told me that I cant stay in the b&b for ever and so I have had to hire a flat to stay in and it is costing me an arm and a leg. Of coarse old Donaldson waited until after I had put the depposit down to say to me that he was sending me out on lone to East Fife and I looked it up on the map Joe and if he sending me out on lone there I woud be as well borrowing your sisters wendy house to live in as it is the middle of no where. But he is just bluffing Joe and I will not be going out on lone to there or anywhere as he does not have a leg to stand on and it woud be as if the Loove had loned the Mona Lisa to the function room at Frankies Bar.

Anyway Joe thanks for getting my some of my money back altho I coud realy have done with the hole lot but I supose you did your best at that and I cant be everywhere at once.

Your pal,

Andy


July 21st


So guess what Joe it looks like I will be going on that holliday after all only it wont be sunny Espanya I will be heading for now but instead it will be sunny Luxinburgh. You probily never heard of Luxinburgh Joe but I have looked it up and it is like Holland exept it is its own country and it does not have a queen like in other countrys but it has got a Duk instead. By now you are probily scratching your head and wondring why I am talking about going to Luxinburgh to meet some old Duk well dont worry Joe I have not gone crazy but the club has got drawed against a club over their called Dude Lang and suddently old Donaldson has changed his tune and says I wont be going to East Fife on lone after all. Well maybe that was news to him Joe but it is no news to me altho I bet at East Fife they have got a couple of defenders who can head the ball without closeing there eyes and at lease a man can probily eat his fill there without the coaches all watching him like a bunch of hawks or saying was that an earth quake whenever he jumps for a header. But I supose at East Fife they try and play the ball on the deck and it is not like here where the midfeilders spend 3/4s of the game jumping up and down on the spot like a Jacks in a box and at half time they turn around to face the other way.

So anyway Joe old Donaldson called me in to his office yesterday and said that they was short of midfeilders now on acct that Brady put his back out diveing for a five pence peace and he said I woud have to go to Luxinburgh even tho it is the same day I was meant to play in Dunoon. Well the people on Dunoon will be disapointed not to see me play but there loss is Luxinburghs gane and Donaldson is making out I am only going to make up the numbers but between you and me Joe if he takes me to Luxinburgh and plays Drummond or Watson or one of them other has beans it will be no suprise to any one if he is out next day selling catalogs door to door only I dont think that will happen Joe as old Donaldson might be stupid but he isnt blind and when he saw me in training today I bet he was already wishing that he had been nicer to me so that when my first book comes out he wont have to spend the hole Satterday hideing from reporters in his basement.

That reminds me Joe I have got some new furnature for my flat as the old furnature is no good and I got a 50 inch tv and a sofa and a kettle and it only had a single bed so I got a king sized 1 as I will maybe need it some day and it cost £800 all inn. It is all good quality stuff Joe but the problem is I am wiped out from the depposit on the flat so if you could loan me 900 pounds against my next wage I would appresiate it. I woudent ask exept I know you got it and you woud get it back strait away only it woudent be for a couple of months till my wages come threw.

Like I say Joe I woudent even ask only we have always been such good pals that have always come threw for each other and the money is as well doing somebody some good for a change instead of just sitting their in your acct collecting dust and if you coud make it a round £1000 Joe that would at lease give me some spending money so that I am not sitting in the house all day like a monkey in his sell. A 1000 pounds is not hardly nothing now a days and I am such a sure thing Joe that the banks woud be at each others throats to give me it and you know you will get it all back as soon as I start picking up my win bonuses which will be when Donaldson stops leting Watson take all the free kicks like he was trying for two points at Murryfield.

Things are going ok right now at the club tho it does not take no Columbus to work out what the problem has been here for the last 10 or 15 years. Their is a lot of older players at the club ie 25+ and maybe they had ambition once but now a days to look at them you woud say they have given up on themselfs and if they was horses Joe you woud not waste a bullet on them. It is like one of those history reenactments they used to do in Selkirk where everybodys dad goes out into a feild and dresses up as Cromwell or whatever only here they are pretending to be football players. They all lie down and die at the end all the same Joe and it is a sad site to see them with there hands on there knees after a run altho to be fair the six billion dollar man woud probily only be worth about £3.50 after Donaldson had finished with him. The only time we get near a ball at training is when we are signing them for charity and I am starting to worry Joe that by the time we play our first game we will all have forgotten what a football looks like and that when the other team kicks off we will jump out of our skins like a cat from a firework.

Well Joe I will need to leave off as the boys told me you can only get in to Luxinburgh if you got the right stamp in your passport and they only does it at the city post office on Mondays so I will need to make tracks. I am not one someone that likes to makes a big song in dance out of every little thing but I guess the people at the post office will want to know what I am going to

Luxinburgh for and they will be in for a big suprise when I tell them I am going to represent our country Joe and not just to take pictures of my brekfast and say what a nice time I am haveing.

Your pal,

Andy

P.S. Joe if you coud send me that 1000 pounds as soon as you read this I would realy apresiate it.

July 22nd

Well of coarse Joe I knowed all along you dont need no stamp to get in to Luxinburgh and I was only going to the post office to pick up some envilopes only while I was their I hapent to let slip that I was going to Luxinburgh and you shoud of seen them at the post office Joe theys eyes was all most poping out of their heads so I guess the boys think they got me a good 1 but realy Joe you can see the last laugh was on them.

You have to get up prity early in the am to get one over on old Andy Fairbairn and from the looks of these guys the only time they saw this side of 12 noon was when the postman needed a signature for there divorce papers.

I am wanting to be at my best for Luxinburgh Joe only the boots my sponser sent me is so small they is like squeezing your foot into a vise and how can anyone play their best when their feet has been aking like that so I went to see the fissio about it today Joe only when I got their Brady was already waiting on acct of his having pulled a shoulder mussel from waveing to his friends or something. So I told him hello and he said whats the crack big man which is a bit rich Joe and abt the same as if a phone box walked up to the empire state building and said hows it going short stuff.

He asked if I was all sorted for Luxinburgh and I says yes and he says good because it is a long trip in to the unknown and you want to be prepaired. Well Joe I already looked it up and it is only a couple of hours on the plane so I says that to Brady and he says yes but that was before the war and now all theys air ports are blowed up and the only way to get their is by steam bote so it will take a bit longer but you will be safe as houses so long as the Luxinburgh navy dont see you. Well Joe it seems to me that there navy shoud be on our side and I said so to Brady and he says yes you woud think that but its every man for himself over their and you cant trust nobody and even the coach driver is libel to be 1 of the Duks sekrit agents and drive you over a cliff.

Well Joe I dident say anything for a wile after that and then Brady says well there is no point in worrying yourself about it the steam botes home are reglar as clock work twice a week and so long as you dont do anything stupid like beat them you will be back next Tuesday before you know it. I am only sorry I wont be fit to go he says I would like to tell my grand children I took a risk once in a wile instead of just staying at home watching Top Gear.

So the fissio looked at Brady after that and said he woud be out for 2 or 3 weeks and then he looked at my feet and said that they was OK but they dont feel OK to me Joe and if that is all it takes to be a fissio I coud probily become a brain surgin inside a week sints all you got to do is look at people whos arm is hanging on by a thred and tell them they are fine but they coud stand to loose a pound or 2. I been feeling weak all day Joe and it is probily from hunger but try telling that to a fissio who thinks a man is OK to play that has got feet like a bag full of broken glass but that someone else is enjured that probily all they has got wrong with them is a stitch in theys side from laughing at cat videos.

So you see Joe it is looking 50 50 that I wont be going to Luxinburgh after all thanks to my feet and I already said that I was playing in Dunoon so it woudnt be fare to let people down now and I am not worried for myself Joe only the squad has got no depth this year so if I was to get blowed up in Luxinburgh it would be goodnight vienner for the hole season and if Drummond and Brady was back running around midfeild the fans woud not know if was Sky Sports they was watching or Scooby Doo.

Your pal,

Andy

P.S. Joe they was a mistake with the money order you sent I only got £800 pounds when it is a 1000 I asked for and if you are sending the extra 200 coud you make it a round 250 and I will owe you it back.

July 24th

Joe you have herd of them places in Swisserland where people that is seriesly ill are aloud to go to die well they could save themselfs the plain fare and just come to our training ground on a Wensday afternoon and they woudent even have to wait until they was ill first. They say a bit off hard work never killed anyone Joe and I guess old Donaldson has got a reserch grant to find out if it is true and all he has got us doing all day is running and jumping and the only time we get anywhere near a ball is when Donaldson balls at us to pick up our heals. That is just a joke Joe but all jokeing a side it looks like old Donaldson wont be happy until I am in my grave and even then he will be standing over me shouting knees up knees up.

I been to see the fissio again Joe but it dident do no good and I cant help wondring what the owners woud make off it if they coud see how there investment was being treated because I dont know much about horses Joe but I do know that if you spend 1000s of pounds on a horse then starve it half to death and ride it round the car park with no shoes on shouting giddyup then its not going to win you no Grant National. It seems to me like busness men is meant to look after there assets but I guess some people is so rich they dont care about money only I dont think that is true in this case Joe and if you seen the win bonuses we are on for the season you woud not supose their is to many fights brakeing out over the check when the owners meet up for lunch.

Well Joe we is off to Luxinburgh tomorow and it looks like I am going after all so I guess it is too bad for the people in Dunoon and I hope the boys remember to leave the bus pointing the right direction when they get off in Dunoon because they will be getting back on it again in a hurry once the supporters see I am not playing. Only by then we will be on the ocean so I supose at lease I will finely get some rest so long as old

Donaldson cant find any hills on the steam bote for us to run up or oars for us to row.

Your pal,

Andy


July 25th


Well Joe their is some reglar comedians on this football club of mine altho I guess that is no suprise to anyone who seen the league table last season and if you watched them running there short corner routeen you woud be doubled up with laughter for $\frac{1}{2}$ an hour only it is a shame they cant stick to the slap stick stuff because some of us is too wise to fall for there tricks even if they make out as if they fell for it just to help keep moral up.

Of coarse I knew all along we are getting the plane to Luxinburgh Joe only I dident let on to anyone and so just for fun I asked Donaldson at the team meeting what kind of food they woud be giveing us on the bote and he fell for it like a sucker and he said we is not getting no bote to Luxinburgh their is no lodeing cranes strong enough to lift our midfeild on board since they stoped bilding destroyers on the Clyde and anyway we are afraid that you will dive for a sandwich someone throws away in the dineing room and we are too busy working with the boys on set peaces to teach them how to breath underwater.

Well I seen what he was getting at Joe and I woud of took a swing at him myself if he wasent so old and I supose little shrimps like him might of been able to get by in football back in the days when people shook hands after every tackle and lifted there caps at a goal but its a mans game now Joe and you got to have a bit of weight behind you and if a little guy like Donaldson was playing midfeild now a days the first sholder charge would be like he was getting fired out of a canon and if it was big McAteer or someone like that by the time he came back down to earth he woud need to learn Japanese just to know which bus to catch. Well their is no danger of that with me Joe and if McAteer came running in to me we both know who would get the worse of it only he would have to text me once he had started his tackle so I woud know not to get bored and walk away.

Well anyway Joe we got to Dood Lang fine and it is as if we had walked off the plane and into a black in white film. Everyone here is gray and all the bildings are gray and the hotel is gray and even the sun in the sky is gray and when Dood Lang come over to us next week and see a red car driving a long or something I supose they will call up the drug testers and tell them that someone has spiked there drinks. We just come back from seeing there stadium and if you think the grounds in the Borders are small Joe well you have got another think coming and the boys and I was sitting in the dug out for 20 minutes before we realise it was the mane stand and when we are coming out on to the pitch before the game we will have to come up the tunnel 1 by 1 and sideways.

Well Joe I will have to leave off and get some sleep as Donaldson told us there fans might camp outside the hotel and try to keep us up but I herd someone slamming a car door about 1 hour ago so I guess the worse is over by now.

Your pal,

Andy

July 26th

Well Joe we are haveing brekfast at the hotel before we head home and you will all ready have seen what hapent last night but they have run out of bacon at the brekfast buffay so I supose I will write and let you know what hapent wile I am waiting for more bacon to come out and their will be no prices for guessing that this brekfast buffay has been the highlight of my entire trip so far Joe and that the runner up was stubbing my toe on the bed side cabanet.

Well Joe ever sints we got to Luxinburgh my feet has been 100% better and it just goes to show you Joe that the fissio dident know what he was talking about an probily it was him pokeing at them that hurt them in the 1st place and you shoud never trust anything a doctor tells you Joe and from now on if a doctor says to me that the grass is green I will be out on the lawn with a color chart to check. Drummond was telling me that in China the doctors stick needles in your feet to fix them and of coarse I know he was only jokeing Joe but it makes as much sents as anything our fissio came up with and I woud sooner have Jack the Riper let loose on me while I was a sleep than let our doctor get his mitts on me again.

But the point is Joe that my feet have been feeling fine and I have been telling Donaldson that sints we got here only I forgot that unless it is to do with pigon racing you might as well be talking to a brick wall and everything I told him fell on def ears because when the team sheet went up in the changeing room I was on the bench and I never got off it Joe not even when it was 0-0 with 2 minutes left and everybody out there was ready to lie down and die. Donaldson said he is saveing me for the 2nd leg only if he had put me on woud not be no 2nd leg Joe as they was only little guys and if I had got on it woud have been a blood bath and there manager woud still be saying there there and trying to cokes them out from under there beds with a plate of custard cremes.

Well Joe thats us leaveing for the airport and you can bet I wont be sorry to get back to Scotland before I forget what noise sounds like and I dont know if you watched it on tv Joe but at the end of the game their was a kind of russeling noise all around the ground and I asked one of the stewarts what it was and he said that was there fans were cheering and I said oh yes I have herd librarians cheering like that when a jakie walks in to the Mitchell.

Your pal,

Andy


July 29th


Well Joe old Donaldson has gone and pulled another

1 of his excapades on me and it is getting to be just 1 thing after another and every time I walk in to his office I think Jeremy Beedle is going to bust out of the cubburd laughing and saying what a good sport I have been.

I dont supose you know anything much about professhunal football Joe but in the proper leagues their is only training three days of the week and the other two days the players get to go off to the horse races or the car deelership altho you are aloud to just stay at home if you get a note.

Well Joe after training today I was talking to the boys about what I will be doing on my days off when old Donaldson overhears me and he says well whatever it is you plan on doing I hope it is something you can get a national certifikit in otherwise you are going to look mighty strange doing it at collage and I says what do you mean and he says we got a deal with the local collage to send our young players there so that if any of them drops out of football they have got something else to fall back on and I says that is fine for the other players but for me it is a waist of time to go to collage and he looks at me and says well in this case I am enclined to agree with you but that is club polissy. So that is that Joe I will be starting collage next week and I will be their two days a week doing busness and admin only I dont see why no teecher at some collage shoud know more about busness than I do and probily they will know quite a bit less and the hole thing makes about as much sents to me as if someone was to hire a driveing instructor to give them judo lessons.

Well Joe I woud not blame you for wishing you was me instead of being stuck in Selkirk looking out your bedroom window and wondring if the next bus going passed will be the 72 or the x95 but you can see that the life of a professhunal footballer is a lot harder than it looks and we maybe get payed a lot of money Joe but we earn every £ and dont get no days off exept Sunday and even then I will lieing down from carrying a whole team on my back. Only their is no chance of me getting any rest in this house Joe wile the people upstairs is carrying on the way they do and if you saw me lieing in my bed trying to get some sleep at 4 in the am wile they are up their reeanacting Peril Harbor I guess you woud think the only upside is that at lease their is no danger of anybody killing me in a jealus rage any time soon.

Your pal,

Andy


August 3rd


Well Joe I have always said that a brane is a terrible thing to waste and seeing as I have chosen to spend mine on football I dont see what busness it is of Donaldson or anyone else to make me go to collage and learn abt stuff that is no use to me just so my brane will be too tired to think of football. If you think about it Joe you woud not expect an Olympic runner to be on his feet in a kitchen all day then go and run a 4 minute mile so why woud you turn round and tell someone who is going need all there mental stamina for football that they have to spend 2 days a wk in collage lerning about spread sheets. It doesent make any sents to me Joe and the fact that Donaldson thinks it is a good idea shows you that if anything he is the one who shoud be getting a bit of education as even a 3 yr old coud see that if somebody is good at eg playing the guitar you shoud just leave them alone and not go trying to teach them to sing as well.

The collage is OK I guess and the canteen is better than ours and it has a pool table and a foosball table so it is not all bad and instead of sitting in a classroom we are in a lecture hall which sounds like a place you woud go to get a telling off eh Joe but actually it is a big room with seats going up like a football stand and a woman stands at the front and talks away about documents and tax brackets and all this other stuff you are never going to need to know until your head is so sore that you can hardly even see the white board. Then in the pm just to change things up a bit there is a man who talks about documents and tax brackets only it is a bit more light hearted this time Joe as he has a cardigan on. Everybody else in the lecture hall is writeing down every little thing the man and woman says as if it is the Bible but personly Joe I have not heard a thing that was worth remembering never mind taking a note of exept where the toilets are and what time is lunch.

I dont know if there are any other footballers in the class but to look at them I shoud say not as it is a sorry crowd Joe and I have to hang back when class goes in in case anyone watching thinks I am heading in to the national geeks convention. There are a couple of girls in the class that are quite easy on the eye Joe and even the lady teacher is all right if it comes to that altho she is maybe about the same age as your mum Joe and she even looks like her a bit. But there is no point in talking to them Joe sints whenever I try all they talk about is busness management and so haveing a conversation with them is a bit of a busmans holliday so to speak.

It seems to me Joe that going to collage is a complete waist of time altho that is only one mans opinion of coarse and I supose it at lease helps keep people in a job who is not kitted out to face the real world. It is only 2 days a week I guess and I do not have enough money to do anything else right now and all I am doing these days is staying at home and watching challenge tv as it is the only channel I can pick up but it is starting to get me down a bit Joe and who woudent be after watching all these people getting realy exited about winning a video player. It kind of makes you feel as if it is all a bit pointless Joe and that everything you are working realy hard towards will be worth 0 in the long run and I keep thinking of all these Bullseye winners sitting there in their liveing rooms now with their steam irons and there cordless phones pretending they are liveing the good life and it seems like the whole thing was just a joke at there expense. But I shoudent complane Joe as I am on Easy St by comparison and I know there are a lot of people who woud give there right leg to be in my shoes but it just seems a bit pointless if it is all going to come to 0 in the end that is all.

Your pal,

Andy


August 5th


Well Joe when you 1st told me all abt your going to

collage I have to admit it sounded like a bit of a joke and I guess it is ok to say that now as it has been 2 years and I never seen you doing any graffic design yet. Maybe it all depends on what you are studying Joe and with some things you will all ways be on a hideing to 0 but with other subjects there is real demand and the more I find out abt busness managment the more I think it is a shame that I turned out to be so good at football as the world of busness is realy missing out and I only wish their was some way I coud combine the 2 skills like a player/busness manager role so to speak. I am only jokeing abt that Joe but they say football is a busness and it will never hurt any football club to have another person around who understands the figures and is able to tell them where they are going wrong eg if the club put ticket prices up 100% they woud only need 50% the attendences to brake even and anything more woud be net profit for the club. It is all about the bottom line these days Joe but if you looked at some of the wages some of us is on here you woud think that the charemans busness strategy involves the jumble sail at the parish church every 2$^{nd}$ Sunday.

I have been thinking abt writeing up a busness strategy of my own for the club and if I was able to save money from other parts of the club that coud be plowed directly into the team itself everyone woud benefit as their is no point in having kitmen and goalkeeping coaches and what have you if you dont have the product on the feild. The truth is Joe my finances have gone down the toilet sints I got here and I have already spend my next 2 wages and then I owe you £800 pounds and a couple of other people have got there claws in to me as well and it seems like the only way I can get back on track is for someone with a bit of busness sents to fix up the finances at the club so that the players is at lease able to have 1 sq meal inside them when they go out on to the feild and not be stuck at home wondering if moldy bread is still moldy once you put it in the toaster.

I will let you know how I get on Joe and I bet if the folks at Selkirk saw me drawing up a busness plan for a top football club they woud not be able to believe it and I guess they will all feel prity silly now after kicking up all that fuss abt petrol money. You have got to spend money to make money Joe and if the people at Selkirk dont believe me they can just ask Mr Smiley at Cardonald Collage.

Your pal,

Andy


August 6th


Yes Joe I know it is a £1000 pounds I owe you and not £800 but I was counting the money as 2 seprit lones and I was only mentioning the biggest 1 and its just as well I did sints judgeing by your reaction if I had said I owed you £200 pounds you woud of hit the roof and I guess I did not think I needed to acct for every last penny to my oldest pal who I have always been their for threw thick and thin which I guess some people woud say is worth more than money at that but I wont quible with you Joe and if you say it is a £1000 pounds then I will take your word for it.

I have sent my busness plan away to the chareman a ½ hour ago Joe and he hasent got back to me yet but it is quite a hefty tomb so to speak and their will be a lot for him to think abt so I guess he will get back to me tomorrow. I wanted to write it in power point like all the busness people do but I dont think I have it on my phone so I have just done it in words instead and I know they say a picture is worth a 1000 words Joe but they woud change there tune if they coud see what I have written altho it woud have been nice to have put in a couple of pictures just to keep peoples intrest up and I tried to put in a drawing of a £ sign but I dont know if you will be able to see it. But anyway Joe let me know what you think and dont worry if you dont have any ideas as it is quite a complicating subject and their are loads of people who have been working in finants for years that has not got the hang of it yet and if you dont believe me just ask the treasurer at Selkirk FC.

"BUSNESS PLAN FOR THE UPCOMEING SEASON BY ANDY JACKSON

As everyone knows now a days football is a busness and to run a successful football club you have got to have a busness plan for off the feild that is as good as your football plan for on it or even better sints a bad business plan can mean that the club goes bankrupped and people wind up in jail or worse wile a bad football plan just means that your set peaces are the laugh in stock of the league and you might as well put your corners out for goal kicks strait away and at lease that way you wont get caught on the counter.

A busness plan can be as complicated or as simple as you like but the best 1s are always simple and the simplest 1 of all is to make more money and spend less eg if every thing at the club costs supporters 10% more then the club will have 10% more income over all which they can then plow strait into the players. This woud improve club moral which woud mean a more successful football club with more supporters and more money. It is a win win situation and it sounds simple when you put it like that but football is a simple game as people say who have never played it and so is busness but the truth is that they are only simple when you know how.

Of coarse if the club has hardly got any supporters

on acct that paying to watch them when you have got a perfectly good cat outside to look at woud be money down the drane there are still other ways to put more money into the playing staff and that is by cutting costs. There are all ways costs involved with running a football club and some of them is worth it and some of them is not and it is down to people with good busness sents to work out which is which. 1 way to do this is to ask your self if the club coud do without some thing and if the answer is yes to get rid of it. For example instead of having people working in the pie shop during the game why not get rid of them and get the stewarts to sell the programmes etc as they have got nothing to do any way. That way the club woud save a lot of money and also the players woud not be disturbed after 1/2 an hour by all the people streeming to the pie shop to get ahead in the cue. It is just something to think abt is all I am saying.

In conclusion the busness plan for this season shoud be to increase sales by putting up prices wile cutting costs by getting rid of all the dead wait. With these 2 goals in mind the busness people at the club will be able to feel as if they are actually doing something useful for the team instead of just standing around in the directors box at half time trying to remember the players names and that is the very simple secret to running a successful football club.

BY ANDY FAIRBAIRN"

Well Joe I am sure that your head is spinning after all that but let me know what you think whenever you can.

Your pal,

Andy

August 8th

Well Joe I never did here back from the chareman abt my busness plan but obviously it has made an impact as old Donaldson took me in to his office this pm and told me I woud be starting agenst Dood Land on Wed. He dressed it up with a load of soft soap abt Europe not being a priority this yr and not wanting his senior players tired out before the season even starts but he said it woud be a good chance to show him what I can do and put myself in his thoughts for the season to come. Well Joe I cannot imagine what old Donaldsons thoughts are like exept maybe the mad bits from Fantasia but I dont supose the club woud of signed me never mind pitched me strait into a big European game if they thought it was eeksy peeksy between me and your auntie in the wheelchare.

So it looks like your old pal Andy came good eh Joe and as a senior player I have got 2 free tickets for the game so if you woud like to come along and see me makeing my big debut I woud be glad to let you have 1 of them for free and if you have any other friends who might want to come they coud buy the other 1 and I will leave them at the ticket office for you Joe and if you just go their before the game and tell them you are a friend of Andy Fairbairn they will know what you mean all right.

Well Joe old Dood Lang will be in for a suprise all right and after what came off in Luxinburg they will probily be comeing here expecting a walk in the park so to speak but they have got another think comeing and when they come out on to the pitch on Wed and see me standing there they will know that this is not going to be no nite at the opera that is for sure.

Your pal,

Andy

August 10th

Well Joe I here what you are saying abt the game and I know it is a long way to travel if you cannot drive but you coud always make a day of it and stay in a hotel afterwards and you are right when you say it will only be the 1$^{st}$ of many and between you and me Joe it will be a long time before old Donaldson dares to leave me out the team again.

But the thing is Joe I might be playing every week from now on but I wont never make my debut more than once and it seems a bit funny that the people from

Dood Lang is comeing all the way over from Luxinburg just to see theys window cleaners getting trampeld all over but my old friend Joe cant make it up as Selkirk is too far away. But of coarse Joe you can only do what you can do and it wont change anything between us old pal if you are not able to make it even tho it will look a bit strange to anybody else.

Well Joe the hour of wreckoning is almost upon us as they say and you probily already seen the big write up abt me in the Daily Record but in case you dident what they said was "BARRY DONALSON IS SET TO HAND DEBUTS TO SEVRAL PLAYERS INCLUDING YOUNG MIDFEILDER ANDY FAIRBAIRN" so you can see Joe that the expectations is already starting to mount and I showed it to Brady at training this am and told him their was a lot of weight on my shoulders and he agreed and said yes and not just on your shoulders either so you can see Joe that even with in the club I am starting to make a name for myself and 1 day their will be a lot of people wishing they had been their for my home debut but I guess family always comes first Joe and I am sorry to here about your auntie.

Your pal,

Andy


August 11th


Well Joe thats fine and I wont expect to see you at the game tonite tho chances are I woud not have seen you anyway as there are libel to be 1000s of fans and to pick anybody out of the crowd woud be like looking for a needle in a hay stack. I guess there will be even more fans comeing sints the game is not on tv for some reason but I am sure the BBC website will be doing live updates or at lease they will put the score up when the game is over but anyway Joe I will try and let you know what has come off as soon as I can.

We have gone over our game plan all week Joe and I am not aloud to tell anybody what it is but obviously I can tell you as who are you going to talk to abt it that is important and anyway we probily wont play like how the game plan says as old Donaldson has got us going into the game like they were world beaters. He is telling us to keep it tight and not to give away no away goals Joe and he has put me in at holding midfeild which is abt the same as hireing the Green Lantern to be your nite watchman and if I am stuck sheilding the back 4 the way he wants me to I will be watching the game through a pair of binoculers. So I wont worry too much abt the plan Joe but I will just play my own game and leave the defending to the defenders.

Well Joe this is the last time you will here from me before I earn my Spurs as they say and I am not a nervous person but I am feeling a bit like it is a big battle I am heading in to and I am just abt to go over the top and no matter how prepaired you think you are you never know what is going to happen next only the one thing I do know Joe is that I will be giving a 110% per cent tonite and if anything goes wrong it wont be down to me.

Your pal,

Andy


August 12th


Well Joe we do not learn abt contract law at the collage until next term but last I heard throwing someone a few coins at the end of the month dident mean you owned them lock stock & barrell and next time you read somebody in the papers saying that players have got too much power give them my phone no and I will speak to them abt it if the cleaning ladies say I am aloud to.

You will probily all ready have seen that we got beat last nite Joe and it was only 1 to 0 but to lissen to old Donaldson tell it you woud think that it was 139 to -12 and that we were not even at the races and he has got the idea in to his head that a draw woud have been a good result but at the end of the day Joe the reason we players are here is to win matches and that means takeing the game to the other team and putting on a show as that is what people pay to come and see Joe and if all we was intrested in was getting a draw we coud just agree that with the other team before the game and not bother playing. Well they was only little guys Joe but they was nippy and they got all the brakes and realy there is nothing you can do about that altho there was no danger of our defenders killing themselfs trying I will say that.

You might have seen the highlights Joe but the highlights dont tell the whole story and altho the result was disappointing I think you have to give credit to our attackers for getting a deal with a so called professhunal football team without knowing what a threw ball is. When you have got support like that around you Joe you have not got a chance and I laid on enough chances to win ½ a dozen games but you woud not have known it if you had been in the changing room at full time and you might have thought that I had killed somebody and maybe I woud have at that if Brady had got gived me a look wile Donaldson was mouthing off and I knew what he was saying was to let it go and that if so much as razed my voice to an old bauchle like Donaldson that is barely held together at the seams I coud wind up answering a murder charge.

So I did not say anything Joe even tho old Donaldson was totally out of line and he made it sound like there goal was my fault for pushing too far forward and he said all sorts about football 101 and complete basics and how naïve I was and how someone who called theys self a professhunal footballer had just been outsmarted by a libary assistant when all that happent Joe was that nobody gived me a shout when I was coming forward with the ball and theys midfeilder got a lucky brake when he tripped over his own feet and run in to me on his way down which I guess is what normally passes for a tackle in the Luxinburgh league and the next thing you know they has broken on us and scored but I dont hardly see how that is my fault Joe as nobody gived me a shout and plus I was still 40 yards away when the goal went in and I do not have no go go gadget legs. But I did not say anything to Donaldson Joe as there is no point and I just waited for him to move on and give somebody else a hard time only it started to seem like it was never going to happen and that I was going to spend the rest of my life being told what a defensive midfeilder is apparently suposed to do but finely he started shouting at someone else altho I noticed that he missed out a couple of people who I supose he thinks put in the performances of there lives. You know me Joe I am not someone that goes easy on themself after a defeat and I guess I coud have played a bit better but it does not hardly matter how inch perfect your passes are when your team mates have got the 1st touch of a stroke victim.

Well Joe we were meant to have the day off today like we always do after a match but old Donaldson called us in this am and had us running again and I mentioned to Brady that even the managers in the Lowland League have got better ideas than to have there creative players running laps only old Donaldson heard me and said well maybe you shoud go back to the Lowland League where you are appresiated and he can say what he likes Joe and he might think that a library asst got the better of me but the Dood Lang manager looked like the little one off the Chuckle brothers so I dont see how old Donaldson thinks he has added anything to his prestige lately and if anything he shoud be looking over his shoulder as their is still plenty of time for the chareman to cut his losses and bring someone proper in before the season starts.

So I guess me and old Donaldson is heading for a show down at some point Joe and he might be used to dealing with players who will sit there quietly and not say boo to a goose so to speak but I am not like that Joe and if I disagree with something I will always say so and he has picked the wrong person to tango with. They always say that when a player falls out with his manager there can only be 1 winner and I guess we have seen from the past that they are rite abt that Joe only this time the winner is going to be me.

Your pal,

Andy

# The End of the
# Honeymoon

August 26th

Well Joe old Donaldson has started up again abt sending me to East Fife and he is menshuning it every other day now only he says he woud be embarassed to send me as I am as it woud be like giving someone a 2$^{nd}$ hand shower curtain for Xmas so he will give me til the transfer deadline to get back into shape as otherwise I woud eat the club all the way down to the Sunday leagues.

Well he is intitled to his opinion Joe but the fact is I only eat what I need to in order to stop from wasteing away and if he did not have us doing 0 but running at training I woud not need to eat ½ so much and if I was old Donaldson I woud not worry my self abt why Andy Fairbairn is eating his fill and instead I woud worry abt why the other players are not eating theirs as the only other way I can see anybody haveing the energy to do all that running if they are on crack cocaine. Some of them look like they have been carved out of wood Joe and when we finish training ½ of them head strait down to the gym so it does not make no sents that they eat hardly anything just a peace of fruit or a little bowl of salad and it woud be like a Formula 1 car running on vitamin c. So you can only wonder what they are doing instead Joe unless you are Donaldson in which case you are counting every spoonful of beans and groneing whenever someone reaches for the ketchup.

We have played a few games sints my last message Joe and against Dundee I came off the bench for the last 15 but I dident get on at all in our next game and I guess old Donaldson must of got a book abt motivation out the Help the Aged shop because he keeps going on abt earning a chance to impress him and grabbing every oppertunity with both hands etc and I guess I am somehow meant to work harder to get in to the team but if I worked any harder at training Joe the next match I would be involved in would be a memorial game and I guess you got to hand it to old Donaldson at that Joe as he is willing to throw the intire season down the drane just to motivate me wile Brady and Drummond are playing like the ball has got a lit fuse attached. I supose old Donaldson knows what he is doing Joe and he has seen enough movies to know that if he puts me in strait off the bat people will see what a great player I am and I will get all the plaudits but if he puts me in bit by bit when people finely see enough of me to make a judgment they will talk abt what a bang up job my manager has done bringing threw such talent. Well Joe in six months time I will have a lot to say to anyone who asks if I am glad to have a manager who looks out for his young players and if they do I will ask them where are all the other young players that Donaldson took under his wing because they are certainly not in the team Joe and if I was going to look anywhere for them it woud be under old Donaldsons patio.

1 thing I have always had Joe is positional sents and wherever I use to play at Selkirk I took to it like a duck to water as I just seem to have a natral understanding of the game and a couple of times I even thought abt trying other positions but it never seemed fare to everybody else. Well I have been giving it a $2^{nd}$ thought lately Joe and if I had it all to do again I woud probily be a goalkeeper as you never seen anyone get an easier

ride in your life. All they do is throw the ball underarm to each other a bit and then practise falling over and our goalkeeping coach is a little old man called Alan who I guess has got too old to have a job with any proper responsibility any more like car park attendent and so they made him goalkeeping coach and all he does is stand there with these big gloves on like he got them in a lucky bag and sometimes he says well done if they get close enough for him to see them. Even old Donaldson never gives the goalkeepers a hard time as I expect he is scared they will bust out crying and I have got a bit more dignity than that Joe but otherwise I woud not mind being a goalkeeper. The money woud not be as good and it seems like I woud have to spend a lot more of it on hair gel but at lease I woud not be watching the whole of my twentys going by in an exhausted haze like a flashback from a prisoner of war movie.

Your pal,

Andy

August 31st


Well Joe you have got to hand it to old Donaldson
and if they gave out medals for self inflicted wounds he
woud have a Victoria cross for cutting off his nose to
spite his face. We are 6 games in to the league season
and I have played exactly 49 minutes of football
includeing injury time and all of it when the game is
rapped up 1 way or another and they might as well be
subbing a penguin on for all the diffrents it woud make.
So far the teams record is 2-2-2 which is abt as average
as it gets and if the bored of directors looked up from
there bank statements every once in a wile and
remembered that they own a football club they woud
be discusted with what is happening as 2-2-2 is ok for a
club as bad as ours but imagine how much better it
woud be if they was playing me from the start instead
of using me as a starter pistol for the supporters 100m
dash to the exit.

I woudent mind so much Joe exept all my money is
locked up in insentives like appearances and goals and

when I put pen to paper I guessed I woud be playing every week and scoring probily every 2nd week and so over the coarse of the season I woud be doing ok but of coarse Joe it hasent been like that and there have been times when we have not even used all our substitutes and you are just sitting their hoping old Donaldson will put you on for the last 2 minutes to get you some extra £ but I guess he must be on insentives too Joe as whenever you are trying to get him to notice you in the last 5 minutes of a game he will look anywhere but the bench but when you are 3-0 up and you scuff a pass it is as if you are the only person in the intire stadium. But I was counting on those insentives to pay back the money I owe people Joe and rite now I am hardly able to cover my expences never mind anything else and I will not tell you how much money I am on as to you it will probily seem like a kings randsom but liveing in the city is a bit more expensive than it is in Selkirk and especially when you are not staying with your parents anymore.

You see Joe football nowadays is to do with image and realy big players make there money threw sponsers rather than their clubs and if you want to reel in the big bucks you have got to have your image sorted out. It is like I have been telling you abt from my collage Joe that you have got to spend money to make money and it is not just the clubs that applys to but every football player is a busness in his own right these days. It is no use to be a good footballer if nobody notices it and if the best footballer in the world was wearing Primark clothes and playing for Hawick Royal Albert the sponsers woud not come near him with a barged pole. Jimmy the asst manager keeps giving me this speech abt what it means to play for such a great club and how there are people out there who woud like to jump on my band wagon and take advantage of my fame only it hasent happent yet Joe and even though I shave every time I leave the house and put on my best clothes just to go across to the Tesco Metro nobody has said so much as a word to me.

I guess maybe the hangers on can tell just from looking that I am not an easy mark and that they woud be as well trying to get blood from a stone but you woud at lease think someone woud ask for my autograph once in a wile and the only time someone has approached me out side of the club has been when I was walking away from the atm and someone came running up behind me and I thought it was a mugger Joe and I was ready to fight for my life but when I turned round it was only some old man chaseing after me with the money I had left in the machine and it is just as well that he did Joe otherwise I woud have been haveing a pint of Tescos chicken stock for dinner. I coud not even afford to give the old man a reward for giving me my money altho I guess it was only 20 yds he had to run so it was hardly out of his way and if I gived him £10 for running 20 yds he woud be on better money than Usain Bolt. So I offered him a ticket to the next home game instead and he turned it down and you might have thought that a homeless person woud be at lease a little excited abt meeting a celebrity but I supose as soon as he realised there was no money in it he lost intrest. He dident even ask who we were playing agenst so maybe he dident know who I was Joe and I guess if he had come to the game he woud not have been any the wiser at that.

Your pal,

Andy


September 8<sup>th</sup>


Well Joe it is only September and Donaldson is already trotting out the excuses abt enjurys exept I guess he has a point as the only thing stopping us from shooting right up the league is that Drummonds hamstrings are ok and Brady hasent broken his leg yet. I am getting my appearance money ok even tho our defence shoud be sued under the trade descripshuns act for claiming theres but the appearance money is hardly anything at all where as the win bonus is £500 pounds a peace for the league and same again for the cups which is a pretty penny when you add it all up. But at lease their is no danger of the club going out of busness any time soon and I bet there has never been a bunch of directors more happy to see there boys get beat as ours and whenever they see old Drummond going up to take a penalty you can practickly see the £ signs in there eyes. Still Joe I shoudnt complane as with all the fines for being late for training etc I am only a couple of win bonuses away from brakeing even for the season.

It is quite hard to explane to someone who doesnt know the 1ˢᵗ thing abt it but our busness teacher Mr Smiley has been teaching us markets and a good market is when people are paying however much things are worth and a bad market is when they dont. I wont embarass you by telling you how much I get paid Joe but it is only maybe 1/2 what a player like me is worth and Mr Smiley calls that an inefficient market tho personally I woud just call it a cheek and how they expect someone to go out there and play there best on a Satterday when they havent been further into the supermarket than the reduced section in abt a month is more than I can figger out.

Anyway Joe I dont mean to confuse you with all this jargin but basicly I have decided to go to the chareman 1ˢᵗ thing tomorow and explane to him about the inefficient market as I expect it will be the 1ˢᵗ he has heard of it and that if he wants to get the best out of me he will need to hike up my wages to what I am worth as there are plenty of other clubs who woud be glad to get me at half the cost altho that is no good to me as it is more money that I need not less so obviously I woud not go.

But the thing is Joe that altho these directors is suposed to be busnessmen a lot of the time they has made there money doing things that a trained monkey could do eg running a pound shop. Well anybody can look at an umbarella and decide that is it worth a £1 but you cant tell how much a football player is worth just by looking at him altho I dont supose there woud be many people humming and hawing over how much to pay for old Brady at that unless it was the people on the anteeks road show. But it is sort of like when we were playing 5 a side up the park and a new kid woud turn up in full kit Joe and you woud always use your chance picking him even tho 9 times out of 10 he was a one man comedy act. Us profeshunals know how to spot a player when we see one and that is what sets us a part but you cant expeck a chareman to know I am worth as much as Brady or Donaldson not unless he has got eyes in his head altho I guess any kind of busnessman shoud know that there is a diffrents between a good investment and money down the drane. Basicly Joe it is all about a thing called appresiation which means that some things keep getting worth more and more and some things keep getting worth less and less and that is what I am going to explane to this old chareman tomorow and it is really in his best intrests to try and listen as otherwise he will be loosing money hand over fist in the long run as they say.

Your pal,

Andy


September 13th


Well Joe I been in to see the old chareman and it is all sorted out with my contract. He is a sharp old fella altho I think he might be a little def as it took 3 or 4 goes to explane to him what I was there for and even then he kept shakeing his head like he dident understand. Well Joe I explained to him all abt the markets and value and efficiensy only he kept tapping his pen on the table and I might have got a bit put off and told him about the farmers market at Kelso instead and how it used to be every second Sunday but I guess the principal remains the same Joe and he seemed to see what I was getting at and finely he said it sounds like you come from a beautiful part of the country young man but I am 82 years old as it is and I wish you woud cut to the chase so I did what he asked Joe and I told him that I dident think we were running an efficient market and that I had come to see abt getting paid what I was worth. Well Joe he laughed like it was the funniest thing that he had ever heard and I guess he is not wrong as most shop assistants woud be doubled up for hours if they seen my contract and he told me that he woud love to pay me what I was worth only the govt woudent allow it due to the minimum wage but that he woud be happy to talk to me again in the summer if I was still at the club. I felt sad about letting the old man down Joe but I told him that I coudent garantee that and he nodded and said no the smart money woud be against it but that it was in my contract that if I make 25 appearances this season I will automaticly get a years extenshun. Well Joe the way things is going with old Donaldson I will be lucky if I manage 25 games of gin rummy and I told the chareman that and he said well that may be but if you are not playing games you are no good to me and I cant go splashing out thousands of pounds on things that is neither useful nor ormamental otherwise my wife woud be out of a job. So I dident say anything Joe and he sort of smiled and said look young man I have a pretty good idea what you are worth to this club but it is no matter what I think it is what Mr Donaldson thinks that counts around here. Lets see where we are in the summer and maybe things will be diffrent then. So you see what he was getting at Joe which is that Donaldson is stopping him from running the club how he wants and he is hoping that some young buck will help get rid of old Donaldson before the summer. Well I have a few ideas that way myself Joe so I thanked the chareman for his time and I got up and left altho I realised afterwards that I had left my notes about market value on his desk and I hope he dident see them Joe as there is some good stuff in there about market efficiensy and Kelso and I woud hate to think of anybody passing it off as there own.

So as you see Joe it is all sorted out and I will finely be safe to put a depposit down on a flat here as I guess that I am here for the duration as they say. I am sorry that I wont be seeing you and Tracy sooner old pal but you will both be able to see me on the tv I supose so it wont be as big a miss.

Your pal,

Andy


September 24th


Well Joe this week in collage I have been finding out abt SWAT analysis which stands for Strengths Weaknesses Oppertunities and Threats. Mr Smiley says a SWAT analysis is a powerful tool any busness can use to see where it is at so I tried doing 1 on myself Joe but I coudent think of any weaknesses and the only threat was that Brady said he is going to smash someones head in if they keep turning all the showers up too hot. So I tried doing 1 on my finanses instead and it is quite a process Joe and not just any old person can do it but writeing down all the Oppertunities made me realise that I have been my own worse enemy in a way and all this time I have been telling you how you need to spend money to make money when realy I have been doing the opposite and even when I have been spending money I have been spending it on things which were not going to get me no place. For example Joe under Weaknesses the first 3 things I put were

*WEAKNESSES*

*Haveing to pay rent*

*Haveing to pay transport to training (dont drive)*

*Haveing to pay fines for being late*

And when you see it layed out in black and white in front of you like that Joe it is obvious what the problem is and you cant believe you dident think of it before but it is realy clear to me now that the only way I am going to get out from under all this debt is if I spend some money and buy myself a house nearer to the training ground. That way I will save on transport and on fines and I wont have to pay any rent and at lease when I was giveing my mum and dad dig money I was getting free wifi out of it.

I have spoken to my landlord abt it and he is not to happy and is keeping my depposit and the next months rent that I had already paid but the fact is Joe if he had been asking for something more reasonable in the way of rent say ½ what he is currently gouging me for I woud probily not have had this brane wave and it shows you Joe that when you have done a busness coarse like I have then you are 1 up on even the most established busness men. Of coarse I will need to get the money together for the depposit on the new house that I am buying but it seems I will have no problem getting a personal lone for that and for the rest of the money I can just get a morgage and the bank will give me the money for free. I guess the bank manager knows that I am someone they will want to hang on to as in a couple of years time I will be swelling there coffers all right and they will have so much money of mine they will need to build an extenshun.

So I am off to see some flats this pm Joe and some of the prices that are being talked abt woud make your eyes pop out and it is a lucky brake for me that the bank will not want there money back for 30 yrs as £100000 pounds will hardly be peanuts to me then altho of coarse it is quite a lot of money to any one at any time in life but I have always said Joe that he who dares wins plus I am sick of liveing in a flat where the shower and the toilet are in two separate rooms as sometimes you need to be able to hop strait from 1 to the other and so if I can get myself that plus a spare bedroom for when my good pal Joe comes to visit I think I will have done prity well for myself.

Your pal,

Andy


September 30th

Well Joe it looks like your old pal Andy is finely on the property ladder and they only had to show me just the 1 appartment before I was in hook line and sinker. It is a real peech Joe and I put my name on the dotty line strait away only it will take a week or 2 for all the paper work to go threw but after that I will have my own 2 bedroom luxury appartment just a few minutes walk from the training ground. When old Donaldson fined me this morning I told him it woud be the last time and he said well no hard feelings and I hope you have better luck in East Fife than you did here and I told him no I wasent going to East Fife but had bought a flat just around the corner and he looked at me and said son I hope either your parents are property magnets or you have just developed a sense of humour because that is the stupidest thing you have done sints you got here and that is reely saying something.

Well Joe if I wanted any busness advice I woud ask Richard Branston or Mr Smiley at the collage not old Donaldson that has never heard the first thing abt investments when what I know abt supply and demand woud make him stand on his head and I woud of told him to stick to what he knows but of coarse that woud practickly be the same as telling him to take a vow of silents and the thing abt people who are ignorent Joe is that they do not know they are ignorent and so they think that they are a world authority abt everything and it is like those players who say they are good in every position on acct they are not reely good at any of them and of coarse I am not getting at you Joe as their were some positions you could actually do OK but on the hole I am just saying that utility players is like those knifes you see on the shopping channel at night that says they can cut threw anything only when you buy them it is like getting blood out of a stone but that is a whole other storey.

Anyway old Donaldson seen that I had got the better of him and walked away only he must have started blabbing abt it the second he got the chance because when we was in line for the shooting drills Brady turned to me and said I hear you got a nice little set up for yourself just around the corner. Well Joe old Brady has got a way of turning things around so that they sound funny even when they are not and so I dident say anything much to him but I told him that I hadent moved in yet and he said oh thats good we will have a house warming party for you when you do if you tell us your address but of coarse Joe I am too wise for there tricks and I told him I had forgotten it and he said well thats okay we will get the estate agent to write it on the label of your duffel coat but the only thing is Joe with Brady yapping at me all the time I dident see what the drill was ment to be and when it was my turn I took a shot instead of a cross and it was a real peech Joe rite in the bottom corner and you woud think that shooting was a more useful skill than crossing the ball and nobody knows better than me that you can put the ball on a sixpence as many times as you like but it is no use to anyone if nobody can finish it at the other end but try telling old Donaldson that Joe he just exploded and started ranting abt not being able to follow simple instructions and then Brady pipped in and said go easy on him gaffer the lad just told me he cant remember where he lives and everybody bust out laughing but of coarse Joe the joke is on them as I know fine where I live and it is 88/6 Princes Street.

Well Joe we have got a big game tomorrow agenst Aberdeen and whatever old Donaldson says I guess he must be impressed by the comitment I have shown to the team so dont be suprised if you see a familiar name scrolling along the bottom of the TV tomorow as I have got a good feeling that I am finely going to get my start and from being on the teamsheet to being on the scoresheet is only a small step as they say.

Your pal,

Andy


October 3rd


Well Joe you probily seen old Donaldson dident start me against Aberdeen and I bet he is kicking himself that he dident as we woud have scored even more goals if he had and in the 10 minutes I was on we scored 2 goals so if you multiply that across the hole 90 minutes it works out that if I had played from the start we would have won 18-0 instead of just 5-1 and you can bet that if we had got 18 goals your old pal Andy woud have had a hand in 1 or 2 of them. As it was Joe it was my throw in started off the move that got us our $5^{th}$ and a lot of people think there is no skill to throw ins Joe but of coarse they woud say that and the secret is that you have got to get the timing right wile people have got there guards down. But that is all by the by Joe as you dont get no assist bonus for actually starting off a move and you dont get no credit either well not at this club anyway and I guess if I sent him a letter from the moon old Donaldson woud hold an open top bus for the guy who licked the stamp.

You might not here from me for the next week or 2 Joe as I just got word that the morgage has went threw OK and my landlord is talking abt sueing me for breech off contract and he is going to get all the utilities cut off which means the phone and the internet so I will probily be going dark for a little wile. But if you are worried abt what is going on with me you will just need to check the Sunday Post under unused subs to see if I am still alive altho there is no guarantee at that sints if Brady was killed in a boating accident he woud still be

the 1<sup>st</sup> name on old Donaldsons team sheet the next
week.

Your pal,

Andy


October 22nd


Well Joe finely your old pal Andy is a property
owner and if I had known what it was going to involve
I might not have gone threw with it but on the up side
it means I have pulled myself up by the boot straps and
got out from the rat race so to speak and if you think of
the number of people who will never be able to buy
there own house never mind do it by the age of 21 Joe
it reely helps to put things in perspective. The only
thing is Joe I dident realise you have to start paying
back the morgage strait away instead of in 30 years and
with that and the lone payments on the depposit it is
going to be a wile before I am treating myself to caviar
and chips.

Having said that Joe I have managed to get off the bench in all of the last 3 games so maybe it is a sign that old Donaldson is starting to come round. Even if I do not get the chance to score any goals I shoud get my contract extenshun no problem at this rate and if not I will at lease have got my name out there on the old flesh market so to speak and just the other day the Inverness manager pointed at me when I was comeing off the pitch so it shows you that I am starting to turn some heads Joe and people are beginning to talk abt me altho I woud not be too keen on going to Inverness Joe as it is almost 4 hours away which is a long time to be on a bus and even longer when your phone rings every 10 minutes with some 1 up the back pretending to be interested in a tobbogan you are suposed to be selling.

Anyway Joe now I have my own place I hope you will think abt comeing up to visit some time altho maybe not strait away as I had to move out of the old flat in a hurry and I left all my furniture their which is good riddance to bad rubbish Joe as it woud have looked like a charity shop clearance sale in my new flat. I do not even have 1 bed right now never mind 2 and I am sleeping on a sofa that I bought from what I thought was a 2<sup>nd</sup> hand furniture shop but I am now starting to think it was an anteek shop and the other day I reached down the back after a £1 coin and I found a newspaper clipping abt Scotland qualifying for the World Cup and I guess if I kept going I might have found the Magna Carter but it is comfy enough for now Joe and I have worked out that if I play 3 games this month I will be able to afford an actual bed and then the place will really start comeing together. It is all very well haveing 2 bedrooms and a living room Joe but if they has not got no stuff in them and you are just walking around this empty appartment you start to feel like you are hideing from the Nazis in WW2.

I have met some of the other neighbours in the starewell Joe and the girl in the flat below is a real honey but she is married just like everybody else in the building and I guess it makes sents Joe as the only way normal people coud afford these flats woud be if there was 2 of them clubbing together. Their is not no Tesco Metro here Joe but their is plenty of shops and take aways and the building is only 2 minutes walk from the traneing ground exept right now it is takeing me closer to 15 as I am haveing to go all the side roads on the way back so that the boys at the club dont find out where I live. There are some proper jokers around these days Joe in case you havent noticed and if some of these boys was as good at football as they are at pulling capers they woud be playing for Paris San German by now plus there are a couple of proper sad cases at the club Joe who have got no friends and will hang on to anybody they can sink their claws in to and it takes enough of my time writeing these emails to you Joe without having another bunch of nobodies dropping round whenever they feel like to tell me abt how funny theys cousins cat is.

Well Joe I guess thats you up to date now exept I forgot to mention I got a letter this morning and it was made out to the "owner/resident" of 88/6 Princes Street and I supose that is me now. Well Joe I wont deny that I felt a little proud of myself when I read that and if I coud send a photocopy to old Mr Milligan at the high school I supose we woud be able to see then who is a clown for not being able to jump higher than

1m 30.

Your pal,

Andy


November 9th


Well Joe they say that professhunal football is like liveing in a goldfish bowl but I dident expect it to start this soon and the only diffrents I can tell is that I supose goldfish get some sleep from time to time without the people upstares carrying on like nobodys busness and if they are reenacting WW2 up there Joe they must be doing the bit when the prisoners of war was tunnelling out of there camps.

So the whole idea of getting to training on time is not reely working out Joe as I am getting kept up all night by the noise and then sleeping in the next day and I set the alarm on my phone but because I do not have no tv or anything else to keep me occupied the charge always runs out and the next thing I know it is 11am and the folks upstares have got out out their shovels and pick axes ready for another day. I did buy an alarm clock but the cord is too short to reach the sofer and even the post man does not wake me up on acct that if he has a parcel for me he just gives it to Mrs Hutchison across the landing as she is never asleep any way Joe and I do not know why she needs a huge 2 bedroom flat to herself when she spends her whole life with her eye pressed up to the sighthole in her door and between old Donaldson at training and Mrs Hutchison at home I feel like I am living my entire life under the microscope.

Well Joe I have got 1 of those little red cards you get from the post man whenever they have left something for you with Mrs Hutchison and I will be honest with you that I can hardly think of anything that is worth going over their for and I sometimes think that this entire flat is just a big pigeonhole for bills. But the onliest thing that is worst than going over to Mrs Hutchisons is her comeing over here and so I guess I will have to go and I hope you will not be offended if you have sent me a flat warming present or something Joe like you said you woud as obviously it will be much appresiated but to be honest with you it is just not worth the bother to me right now.

Your pal,

Andy

November 10th

Well Joe I know I said yesterday that even a present from yourself woud not be worth talking to Mrs Hutchison for but it turns out there is 1 thing that woud be worth going over for Joe and that is a call up to the Scotland U21 squad and in case you havent figured it out Joe that is exactly what it was. The letter was from the SFA and it said to report for training at Hampden on November 21 ahead of the friendly agenst Portugal and not to tell anyone abt the letter as the official squad hasent been released to the press yet but I dident think their coud be any harm in telling my old pal Joe and of coarse I am counting on you to keep the news to yourself Joe but if you do happen to let the news slip anyone in Selkirk just let them know that they shoudent tell any one else.

Well I wont lie to you Joe I am a bit suprised as I did not even know the Scotland manager had been to any of our games and I thought it woud maybe be another six months or so before I was on the radar but at the same time I am not that suprised as now that I have been up close with the so called top players in the league and seen what they have got I am not that impressed. There is definately nobody like me playing in the top division right now and when it comes to midfeilders who can run around like headless chickens for 90 minutes we are spoilt for choice Joe but if they are looking for someone who has got the branes that he was born with and conserves his energy for the right moment their realy is no one else like me.

The only thing is Joe that the SFA want me to bring along proof of identity like my utility bill and that is ok as I have got them comeing out of my ears but they want my passport Joe which I have not seen sints I moved into the new flat and they also want my birth certificate and I am not totaly sure where that is. I know for a fact that I was born at the Borders General Hospital but I guess the SFA wont be able to take my word for it and they will need someone from the hospital to vouch for me. I am not even sure if I had a birth certificate in the 1$^{st}$ place Joe but I supose if the game is at Hampden I wont reely need my passport and if Messi had not had no birth certificate they woud still have found a way to turn him out for Argentina so I shoud not worry myself abt it.

Your pal,

Andy



November 20th



Well Joe I am at the end of my rope here and I tried ringing the phone no on the SFA letter abt my birth certificate but they is no answer and it woud be hard lines if I missed out on the oppertunity of a life time on acct of not having a peace of paper. I tried ringing up the hospital but it was a bad line and they dident seem to understand what I was talking abt and I am almost at my wits end with it Joe and I woud not ask you if it as not a desprit situation but if you could go over to the hospital as soon as possible and maybe even as soon as you read this email and ask them if they can give me a new birth certificate or even just a note saying that I was definately born there it woud realy help me out and if you coud not bother asking the wee specky guy at A&E that woud be even better as I am sure he has got a grudge against me Joe and how was I to know that my leg was not broken Joe I am not no dr of medicine and it was a prity heavy jar of mayonnaise but the point is Joe I reely need that note asap and I will fob them off at training tomorrow but I guess they will definitely want it in time for the game on Sat so if you coud just pop across to the hospital the bus there is prity reglar and it woud save your old pal a lot of stress and worry.

Thanks Joe you are a great pal and when I score my first goal for Scotland I will point to my right hand and you will know that I am dedicating my goal to you as you have all ways been my right hand man only it wont be if I score this Sat as I have already told my mum I will make sure and point to the sky if I score as she says that my gran will be watching down from heaven but if my gran was not watching me that time I got in to the cutlery drawer I dont see why she will be suddenly fascinated by me now that she is dead.

Your pal,

Andy


November 21st


Well Joe you can call off the visit to the hospital as I wont need that note no more and I guess the reason they wanted my birth certificate was to see if I was born a sucker well their is 1 born every minute Joe as they say but your old pal Andy is not 1 of them that is for sure.

I was late getting to Hampden Joe as it is in the

middle of nowhere and they is not even no train station or anything for miles around and I was still not able to get any one from the SFA on the phone to see if I shoud bring my own water to drink or if I woud need to bring a packed lunch but I did my research Joe and I looked it up on Google Maps and there is a big Tesco rite across the road and so I decided just to turn up empty handed rather than spend more money than I needed to and of coarse if it turned out that I was meant to bring my own drink I coud nip over to the Tesco and get something then.

When I got their the lads was already out and training but I coudent see the manager so I went over to 1 of the coaches to say hello and he asked if I was from the newspaper and I told him no I had been called up to the squad and he laughed and said well with fashion sense like yours you will fit rite in. So then I noticed that the players were all wareing blindfolds on theys eyes Joe and the footballs made a noise like there were bells in them and I realised it was the Scotland blind football team and I told the coach that there had been a mistake and that I was here to train with the proper team and he said well we like to think of ourselfs as the proper team and I woud be careful how you use that word as you probily know that blind people have got super hearing and are very sensitive as well but if it is the other Scotland team you mean you are here 4 months early as they are not playing again until Spring.

Well Joe I wasent sure if he was pranking me or not as the blindfolds coud just as easy been a practical joke they do on every new player and I guess some of the Scotland midfeild coud play just as well with a blindfold on as they do without so when I walked away I waited at the gate for a little bit and watched them just to make sure but if they was not blind Joe they shoud get an Academy Award for pretending and the only thing I was not sure abt Joe was that for all theys super hearing when it came to coaches they was just as deaf as any other player.

Well when I got in to training this morning everybody was very quiet until Drummond came in and then he said well theres a sight for sore eyes and everybody bust out laughing all at once which has not happened at training sints the last time Brady tried a rabona and I have herd every joke under the sun now that is to do with eyes or seeing and most of them are not even jokes Joe and dont make no sents and after training Drummond came in to the changing room and said has anybody got some aspirin I have a blinding head ache and I said to him well Drummond that was a good 1 you got me all right and when I get called up to the Scotland team for real I will ask if there is a Scotland team for people with no sents of humour and they will probily make you captain and then the joke was right back on him Joe and everyone else laughed and even he coud see that there was no answer back to that.

So that is the storey Joe and I guess everyone else at the club thinks I shoud have been wise enough to see that it coud not have been a real call up but it is them I feel sorry for Joe if they are liveing in a world where the only way they will get a call up to the Scotland squad is if someone plays a practical joke on them and they might have given up on thereselfs Joe but I havent and if you cant hope that 1 day someone will recognise your talents what are you even still playing for.

Your pal,

Andy


December 10th


Well Joe I am starting to think that this hole football
club is just a goverment scheme to get more people
going to collage and if you dont count the Dood Lang
game I have spent less than 90 minutes on the pitch
this season but have been in collage 2 whole days a
week every week for months and I know we used to
complane abt paying subs at Selkirk Joe but what is £2
here or there for a game of football next to hours of
your life spent reading abt busness strategys all so you
can play less than 1 game of football. It doesent add up
Joe and I am getting to the stage now where I woud be
happy if they sent me out on lone to East Fife like old
Donaldson keeps saying they will just so I get to play a
little football in between classes.

The collage is still going ok only I kind of let it slip that I am a professhunal footballer and so everyone treats me like a celebrity now which is a bit embarassing as just because you are good at football doesent make you a better person than anyone else altho I guess my time is worth more money than theirs at that and that is not me being big headed Joe that is just a fact and anyone in busness admin coud tell you that something which is worth a lot of money is a better asset than something which is worth 0. So I guess it is probily only right that people shoud treat me a little diffrently Joe and I am not asking for the red carpet treatment I am only saying that it is good for the collage and for the other students to have someone with a bit of presteege abt them studying here and anybody with a bit of sents woud see that if you have someone in the organisation who is more important than your average Joe you shoud try and keep them happy that is all.

For instants Joe there is this girl Lucy in my classes who hardly ever shows up and when she does is always sitting on her phone cracking wise abt this and that but sints she found out I am a professhunal she has been turning out every week and she is on tentahooks to here all abt how much footballers earn and how much my house cost and all this other busness stuff and it is good to see someone finely takeing an interest in their education Joe and I am not blowing my own trumpet but if it was not for me she woud still be sitting up the back on her mobile phone crying with laughter when Mr Smiley turns up with his jumper on back to front.

But the point is Joe that I am talking and thinking like some kind of collage professor when I shoud be talking and thinking like a footballer which is what I am and it is no good to be spending so much of my life reading and thinking abt things that is not to do with football and I keep having nitemares where I am sitting in my study with my slippers and pipe reading the Sunday papers and thinking abt inflation. I am not learning nothing abt football just from training and if old Donaldson was not allowed to say hows the diet to me I would think he was a deaf mute. It is all very well for him to say that I am doing well and that he will maybe give me more of a run out going forwards but it will be no good to me Joe if I am just skin and bones by then and there are times when I am so weak with hunger that I can hardly lift the fork to my mouth.

Well Joe the transfer window is abt to open and I am thinking abt calling old Donaldsons bluff and asking for a transfer to another club if he will not start giveing me some game time and he can huff and puff abt East Fife all he likes but we both know that I woud get snapped up by another premier league club in a heartbeat Joe and it is not so long ago that I was being talked abt in connection with a Scotland call up and it woud be a good idea for some folks around here to remember that.

Your pal,

Andy


December 20th


Well Joe training this morning was the same old death march as always and I had just abt made up my mind to speak to old Donaldson and when I was getting my stuff together in the changing room Brady looked up at me and said whoa reign it in their lightning where are you off to in such a hurry. He said you must have already run abt 200 yds today so be careful or you are going to burn yourself out. Well Joe I told him I was going to see old Donaldson and ask him for more game time or a transfer and he looked at me and he said well theirs no accounting for taste and I guess there are plenty of men woud pay good money for what you are abt to get for free but all the same I woud think abt what you are doing if I were you and I said to him well I have had plenty of time to think abt it wile I have been kicking my heels on the bench all season a football career is only so long and I have already spent most of mine warming up and Brady says you are right that a football career is short but yours will not get any longer for crossing old Donaldson and I have seen dozens of young lads like you come threw the club over the last few years and most of them have come to 0 but old Donaldson seems to be warming to you for some reason and I guess you must remind him of a golden retriever he had when he was a boy but I know for a fact he is planning on giving you a decent run out agenst Motherwell on Sat so if you can manage to keep your big cakehole shut until then you will be glad you did.

Well Joe I dont know where Brady gets off with all that cakehole stuff as I can hardly afford a cake of soap these days but I woud prefer not to have to move to another club on acct I just bought this flat near the training ground so unless some other club is willing to offer me a lot of £££ to move I woud probily rather stick where I am so I decided not to go and see old Donaldson but to put the ball in his court as it were and see what he does. To me a good run out means at lease ½ an hour as that is all I need to show what I can do tho of coarse it is putting the pressure on a bit Joe and reely people shoud wait until the end of the season to judge. But try and tune in to the 2$^{nd}$ half of the Motherwell game on Sat Joe as their is probily no point in watching the 1$^{st}$ half.

Your pal,

Andy

December 24<sup>th</sup>

Well Joe I dont know if you seen the Motherwell game but if you did you woud probily think I went in to the changeing room and got a standing ovation after my tackle on Fowler and nearly scoring that free kick but you woud of thought wrong Joe and you might not have guessed I was walking strait in to a 30 megaton blast from Donaldson but that is exactly what it was.

I was not anywhere near our goal when they scored there equaliser Joe but Donaldson seemed to think it was my fault anyway and as soon as I walked in to the changeing room he said I dont know how you managed to get Motherwell FC in the secret Santa son but you are only meant to spend £10 max and that point you just handed them cost us a lot more than that. So I said to Donaldson I wasent anywhere near the goal when it went in and he said yes and that is exhibit B but 1<sup>st</sup> of all I woud like to know who taught you to go for goal from a free kick when you are 1-0 up in enjury time and everyone is telling you to play it short and I said I dident hear them and then Brady butted in and said I guess when you saw we had a free kick within 25 yards the sound did not have time to catch up with you and I have not seen you run that fast sints that burger van pulled up outside our training ground but old Donaldson ignored him and said well we have got it on good authority that you are not blind and you certainly always seem to hear the lunch bell alright so I guess that only leaves 1 thing and I said yes that I have got a rent a mouth manager that is not worth listening to and everyone went very quiet.

Well Joe it just seemed like everyone was getting a say exept me and something came over me and next thing I was standing up in the changing room giving old Donaldson a peace of my mind and I told him a few home truths abt how to manage a football team and how it was easy to keep putting someone on when the game is mostly over and blameing them for whatever happens but maybe he shoud put himself under the microscope for a change and after I had run out of things to say I walked out the changing room and slammed the door realy hard behind me only it wouldent slam as it has got one of those bits up the top that stops it from shutting too quickly.

Well I was in the canteen for maybe 5 minutes before Brady came along and he said I thought I woud find you here in your happy place and I dident say anything as I was not in the mood and Brady sat down next to me and said well it was good that you got all that off your chest and you certainly look a lot happier for it but the only thing you coud of done that was dumber than that free kick was shouting at Donaldson. So I started to say something Joe but Brady cut in and said you might not think Donaldson likes you but take a look around the changeing room if you are ever allowed back in and count how many other 20 year olds are in the squad and you will see that Donaldson does not fall over him self giving youth a chance and he must think very highly of you to make you the only exeption. So I says to Brady well he treats me like dirt and Brady says he is a bit hard on you sometimes but I guess he thinks he is putting himself out on a lim by haveing you in the squad and it makes him look prity bad when you pull boneheaded stunts like you did out there today but the mane thing is that we have all had our run ins with Donaldson and you just have to ride it out and not do anything else too stupid for the next couple of years and I guess I coud kind of see the sents in what Brady was saying Joe and I told him well I am prepaired to forget all abt it if he apologises and Brady laughed and said there is a lot of people down the job centre who are waiting for Barry Donaldson to say sorry so I woud not hold your breath but maybe you shoud just go home and forget abt it all and see how the land lies on Monday.

Well I have went home Joe and I have tried to forget abt it but it is easier said than done and I wish I had been able to come down to Selkirk for Xmas but of coarse that is out of the question wile we have still got games and training on and if I do hand in a transfer request on Monday Joe I will maybe menshun on it that I would like a club a bit nearer to home and I am not sure where Falkirk is but I know old Dougie used to drive up there for work so I guess it cant be too far.

Well Joe Merry Xmas.

Your pal,

Andy


December 27<sup>th</sup>


Well Joe I went in to training this morning in the spirit of charity ready to forgive and forget as they say and instead of that I got it throne back in my face and I guess this means it is all out war between me and Donaldson now but anybody who heard my side of the story woud be 100% on my side and here is how it all came out.

I coudent manage to sleep last night what with 1 thing and another and I wound up spending half the night watching the ping pong championships on tv and you woud think that woud be enough to put any body to sleep but the funny thing is Joe it kind of hypnotises you watching this little white ball bouncing around and when they get in to a proper ralley like some of the Chinese ones do you start to forget that you exist and it is quite strange Joe and it made me feel like I was a little ball being bounced between Brady and old Donaldson in a ralley that goes on forever. So it dident help take my mind off things at all and by the time it was finished and then the volleyball after that it was abt time to get up anyway so I headed in to traneing early to see if we coudent maybe sort this thing out.

I know it is not easy to apologise Joe as I have seen how hard lots of people seem to find it so I thought it woud be the right thing to do if I went in early so old Donaldson coud apologise to me in private and by the time everyone else showed up the 2 of us woud be all smiles and everyone else woud be left scratching there heads and wondering what the hell was going on. But of coarse you try and do a nice thing for someone and they throw it back in your face and when I walked past old Donaldsons office on my way to the changing room he dident say anything and so I made out I had forgot something and went back past again and finely old Donaldson looked up and said if you have got something to say to me son come in and say it only stop waring out my brand new carpet so I stopped in the doorway as if I hadent seen him and I said oh I dident see you there I just came in early to get a bit of extra training in and Donaldson said yes I can see that and you must have done abt 100 laps of the corridor already and I started to explane Joe abt keeping on leaving things in the car but then I remembered I havent got a car and anyway Donaldson cut me off and told me to come in and he pointed to a seat and I sat down.

So then Donaldson says look son I hate to see a dumb animal in pain and you are obviously suffering real bad so why dont we just put this all behind us with an apology and I said yes that woud be fine and there was a long pause wile we looked at each other and then Donaldson said well I applaud you for retaining a sense of humour in the face of tragedy but this is you on your $2^{nd}$ strike now and it is time to man up and take some responsibility for yourself and I still dident say anything and finely he sat up in his chare and said well that is quite a storey you are taking down to the reserves with you son only dont expect no one to be impressed by it because our reserves is full of players that were doing quite well for themselfs until the day they gave Barry Donaldson a bit of back chat so you can jog on down the corridor and clear your locker as you will be training on the back pitches for the next wee wile.

So I went and got my stuff Joe and now I am training with the youth team as we cant afford a reserve team and Donaldson only said all that abt the reserves because he knew it woudent make any sents if he was only talking abt the youth team but he can talk all he wants Joe and I remember my dad used to be like that too and if he had done something wrong by you he woudent know what to do exept to keep piling it on until things had got so bad he woud have to do something realy nice to make up for it like take you to McDonalds and obviously I dont want old Donaldson to take me to McDonalds but I guess if I let things get bad enough eventualy someone will have to step in to fix them and wether thats Donaldson or the chareman or the players associashun I dont know but 1 thing I do know is that I have got something big comeing to me for everything I have had to put up with at this club so far.

It is at times like this that I wish I had an agent Joe and if we was not off collage for the holidays I woud ask Mr Smiley to be my agent as the stuff he knows abt the law and what you are aloud to get away with woud make your head spin. I have heard that the going rate for agents is they get 10% of everything you make which seems like a bit of a rip off as they are not doing 10% of the work or anything like it and if I ever get an agent Joe you can be sure I will be haggling him down to 5% altho if you are able to argue your own agent down to half his wage it woud maybe not say much for him as an negotiater Joe and the last thing I want is to have someone else monkeying around with my career and if all I want someone to go in to Donaldsons office and agree with everything he says I coud find plenty of candidates around the changeing room who woudent even ask to be paid for it.

Your pal,

Andy


December 30th

Well Joe I have been training with the under 20s the last couple of days and to be honest with you it has been a breath of fresh air as the youth coaches actually do work on tekkers and skills and so on instead of just jumping and running all day long. It is hard to get to know anybody here as they already have there little cleeks and all they talk abt is what happened when they played Raith Rovers u20s etc and to someone who has played in European competition it is funny to hear them banging on abt big games against Alloa and Stirling Albion but I dont want to say anything Joe as it woud brake there spirits and I guess now that I am here I am kind of there leader altho no one has said wether I will be captain or not. You remember how old Knoxy at Selkirk use to say that haveing an arm band isent what makes you a captain and he was right there Joe altho he was wrong when he said how everybody is a captain as that doesent make no sense as you can only have 1 captain at a time and if you have got a team of players and 1 of them has played in the Europa league and the others all still talk abt being the best player at their school I guess it does not take no brane of Britain to work out who the real leader is Joe even if he doesent have no arm band.

Of coarse Joe it is all academical seeing as I wont be here past January 1$^{st}$ when the transfer window opens. Last night I sat down and wrote my official transfer request and I left it on old Donaldsons desk this morning when he went out to the toilet and this is what it said:

*Dear Mr Donaldson*

*I woud like to inform you that I am handing in an official transfer request and here it is.*

*I have enjoyed my time at the club but I feel that my relationship with management has broken down to the exstent that it is affecting my developement as a footballer. Tho I am greatful to your self and all at the club for giveing me this oppertunity I feel that the time has come for me to further my career elsewhere preferably somewhere that is quite near my flat.*

*I do not know how you do it nowadays but I remember people used to talk abt faxing players details to clubs exept I dident* never see a fax in the front office and I am not sure if people use them now but I woud be very greatful if you could notify other clubs who might be intrested that I am now available for transfer exept coud you not tell Inverness as it is too far away and not Ross Country either as I do not know where it is but I bet it is miles away and do not bother sending it out to teams that has never been in the 1$^{st}$ division as I do not want any time wasters.

I hope the club gets a decent transfer fee for me to reflect the time and effort you have put in to my developement over the last 6 months. I am very greatful for the clubs faith in signing me and without your support I do not know where I woud be right now maybe somewhere a lot worse but then again maybe somewhere quite a bit better. I guess we will never know and their is no point in going down that road.

Again I woud like to say how much I have enjoyed my time at this club and it will always have a special place in my heart and no matter where I end up in the world they will always be the first results I look up in the newspaper altho obviously if I am in Italy or Spain or somewhere they woud not bother to have there results in the newspapers there as it woud not mean nothing to them.

Let me know if their is any interest and best wishes for the *future.*

*Yours*

*Andy Fairbairn*

What do you think of that Joe I bet it made old Donaldsons ears burn just to read it and all that stuff I said abt being greatful was just a load of nonsents but you have got to put these thing in to a goodbye letter so that anyone who reads it thinks you are comeing out on top. The only thing is Joe that their was a couple of other things I forgot to menshun in the letter and so I had to write another 1 and leave it on old Donaldsons desk 2 hours later and it said

*Dear Mr Donaldson*

*I hope this letter finds you well and that you have had time to discuss my previous letter with the chareman. Their was a couple of things I forgot to menshun in my other letter tho and I just wanted to let you know.*

*1$^{st}$ thing is that I have got next to 0 money and so I cannot go to any club that wants to give me even less money than I am on right now. I dont know which clubs pay good money so I will leave*

*that up to you to decide. Plus I have herd that when a footballer moves team he is intitled to a % of the transfer fee and I think around 10% woud be fare and woud let me get my head above water for a little bit.*

*Also if you have any contacts abroad I woud be willing to move overseas so to speak only it woud have to be to a country where they all speak English. I woud also be willing to go to France as I did French at standard grade and I was quite good at it only my teacher always used to mone abt me saying my French with a Scottish accent but if that is just your natral accent that you were born with I dont supose their is anything much you can do abt it no matter how many detenshuns they give you. I woud also be happy to consider moveing to Newcastle if they were interested.*

*Best wishes*

*Andy Fairbairn*

So that is it Joe the dye is cast as they say and I will just need to sit back and wait for the offers to come flooding in and if I do get offered the chance to go to a club in Europe I will put in a good word for you old pal and see if I can get you along for the ride as quite often when clubs abroad sign a player they will also sign his little brother or somebody else like that who is obviously no good and never going to make it but they sign them any way just to keep the mane player happy. Imagine me takeing in the sun and sites at Monty Carlo with my good pal Joe well thanks to old Donaldson we are already halfway their. A bien toe Joe.

Tonne amie,

Andy


December 31st


Joe

I have been sent on lone to East Fife.

Your pal,

Andy

# Back to Basics

January 10th


Well Joe I dont know if you have visited East Fife before but I guess there is as much point asking you that as asking if you have been to Narnia or Never Never Land because it turns out they is no such place and the people at the train station were pooling faces for abt 20 minutes before someone else in the cue got mad and told them East Fife is in a town called Methel. Well it seems there is no trains in Methel Joe so I had to get the bus and it takes 1 ½ hours to get there and when you add in the travel expences it starts to look like a prity bad deal for me old pal and when I was in the deepo waiting for the bus to come I looked at the homeless people sitting in out of the cold and I wondered what theys lifes must be like but at this rate I wont have to wonder much longer Joe and before long I will be looking forward to the 3 hours on the bus as the only time during the day that I can have a seat without someone with a walkie talkie telling me to buy some thing or get out.

I do not want to disrespect my new fans Joe and so I woud not say this in public but I do not see why anyone woud think that Methel is worth a 90 minute bus journey. I had a bit of a walk round once I got there as I couldent find the stadium and I was scared to ask anybody as you cant see there faces Joe on acct they have all got their hoods up like the sand people from Star Wars but from what I saw their is not much to write home abt. I know Selkirk is kind of a dump Joe but this place makes Selkirk look like the Ritts and it is suposed to be by the seaside but when I went down to the harbour the water was this thick grey stuff like when people make jelly but forget to put the colour in and if Jesus had walked on water in Methel the only wonder woud have been that he diden't catch rabies.

Well finely I got to the stadium Joe and you can see why East Fife is in the third division as there ground looks like something your granddad used to build out of matchsticks. You probily know all abt this Joe as you have been around the block when it comes to little teams but most of them train during the evening as theys players have got to have jobs outside of football and what with 1 thing and another I was a bit late and the 1st team were gone by the time I got there. The youth teams were still training tho and the coachs said I coud join in so I did a bit of ball work etc with them. They were only 15 and they were not up to much and if they were not as bad as the players at Selkirk it is only because they have not had the same amount of practice and give them a few more years of training like this and they will be able to shank a long pass strait in to the stands with the best of them.

After we was finished 1 of the coaches came up to me with a funny look on his face and asked me what my name was and I told him. He dident look any the wiser but their has been no word of it in any of the papers or anything and I guess East Fife are waiting to make a big announcement and hold a press conference etc so it doesent suprise me that they havent told their youth coachs abt it as if you want some news to get around a football club the quickest way to do it is to take a youth coach to the side and say *this is just between you and me*. But I guess now the cat will be out of the bag and the Methel Advertiser or whatever it is called will be full of nothing else this week.

When I finely got back home I seen that I had a text from Jimmy the asst manager asking why I had not turned up to training at my new club. Well Joe if I had knowed that they was sending me to Timbucktoo on lone I guess I woud have left the flat a bit earlier like say 1998 so I told him that I had some transport problems and that I dont know where they get off sending me on lone to somewhere that has not even got no train station and he did not reply Joe so I guess that shut him up prity good but it shows that they are still thinking abt me Joe and I bet old Donaldson is kicking himself as he probily dident expect things to go this far but I am made of sterner stuff Joe and if he thinks I am going to lie down and die on acct of being sent to some 2 bit outfit in the middle of nowhere he has got another think coming. It has only made me more determined to succeed Joe which I guess is the exact opposite of what he had in mind altho between you and me Joe I dont see me sticking it out here for another 5 months as there stadium is a joke and there youth coachs look like the people you used to see waiting for Frankies Bar to open at 8 in the am which woud not be so bad Joe exept so do the youth players.

Your pal,

Andy

January 15th

Well Joe I hope you have not booked a fortnite off work to try and get up to Methel for a game some time as it turns out that the deal is off and I wont be going there on lone any more. The whole thing has been a shambels from start to finish and once you have heard abt the latest shinanigans from Donaldson & co you will think I must have the patients of a saint to put up with it.

So Joe I am on the bus to Methel yesterday pm and I have made a special effort to get their on time so nobody can say anything and it is not even a proper coach with big seats or anything just a normal service bus like the 72 to Bannerfield so all the way their you are stuck looking strait at all these Methel people who have basicly given up on thereselfs. Well Joe I am trying to save the charge on my phone for listening to music when the phone rings and I do not want to answer it but it seems as if it is going to ring forever so finely I answer it and sure enough it is Jimmy the asst manager asking me where I am. Well Joe I tell him I am on the bus to Methel and he doesent say anything for a little wile after that and I am begining to think that he is cut off when he says where the hell is Methel and I tell him that it is a good guess but at lease hell has got central heating and if I had knowed that the place they were sending me on lone was in the middle of nowhere I woud never have agreed to it.

So anyway Jimmy starts talking to someone else and that is something which reely bothers me Joe as why bother phoning someone if the person you reely want to talk to is in the same room as you and all the wile my phone battery is wasteing away and I am just abt to hang up when he says something to me only of coarse you cant tell wether they are still talking to the other person or to you Joe so I dont say anything at 1ˢᵗ until he says Andy are you still their and I say if you mean still on the bus to Methel yes I am and I am looking prity good odds to be on it for another 45 minutes and he says well get off as soon as you can because you are going to the wrong place and I dont know what made you think we was sending you to East Fife on lone when we told you all along that we was sending you to East Kilbride.

Well Joe I dont supose you ever got the bus to Methel before or anywhere exept the 24 hour Tesco but once you leave Glasgow there is nothing but fields all the way to Methel and the bus hardly stops at all so unless I brake out the fire exit and start walking I am not going anywhere but Methel now and I tell Jimmy that and he grones and says you are the 1ˢᵗ player I ever met that has got the same amount of branes in his head as he has in his feet and I supose if we had sent you to Easter Road you woud of turned up in Easter Island but I guess there is nothing else for it exept you miss tonites training and go along on Thursday instead only you will not have done yourself any favors with the folks at East Kilbride and they run a prity tight ship their so you will have to nuckle down and get back in the saddel etc etc and all the wile he is going on and on giveing me his big inspirational speech like he is Jesus on the mound I am sitting their on the bus to Methel looking at this mangy old dog down the front that is watching its owner turn a crisp packet inside out to get to the crumbs and I am wondering why anybody bothers doing anything with there lives and when finely he finishes and hangs up I have got no charge left in my phone so I cant even play candy crush saga and instead I am stuck spending the whole rest of the journey looking out of the window and trying to think of ways that things coud be worse.

I do not think you played against them last year Joe on acct that they was important games and we needed to put out our strongest team but East Kilbride are in the Lowland League same as Selkirk and yes they are top of the league and Selkirk are down at the bottom but I did not go turning my life upside down and moving to the big city just so that I coud be wearing a different colour shirt wile I am getting pumped by Gala

Fairydean. At lease Selkirk has there own ground and so forth but East Kilbride plays in this sort of community centre that is all closed in with fences so that you feel like you are playing against the prison team from Mean Machine and I know it is a bit annoying at Selkirk when the litle kids are playing cuppy behind the goals but at East Kilbride the 10 year old boys are betting each other cigarettes on who is going to be the 1st person from the other team to get knifed. I guess at lease they will be on my side now Joe and maybe I will even get to be there leader if I beat the biggest one in a pit fight but it is not exactly what I signed up for and at this stage I am abt 30 seconds away from getting on the first bus to Selkirk and never coming back.

Your pal,

Andy


January 23rd


Well Joe I finely made it to East Kilbride and if I am

being honest I learnt more abt football sitting on the bus listening to Phil Collins than I have here. The stuff they do is reely basic and it is like that time you got put in the bottom maths class and you spent a whole period writing down the names of shapes. I guess the manager can only do what he can with what he has got and if that means spending 2 hours teaching grown men how to kick a ball in a strait line then so be it but it is not exactly prepairing me for life in the big league.

The manager here is a guy called Mackinnon and he seems ok Joe altho he doesent exactly hate the sound of his own voice and after the 1st session he kept me back to tell me where he saw me fitting in to his game plan and it was nice to get some complements Joe after getting used to nothing but sarcasm but still Joe I am prity quick on the uptake and it does not take 3 hours to tell me when to drop back and when to go forward and by the time he was finished I was beginning to forget that their was a world outside of old Mackinnon and his voice droaning on and on. He is the same during games and he cannot so much as say man on without telling you what the man had for breakfast. I guess he is not doing no harm Joe but it makes you feel as if he won the job in a charity raffle and any minute now he is going to go back to selling ties door to door.

On acct of the mix up with East Fife I have only played 1 game so far Joe and that was against Gretna and I made them look like a bunch of flops as per usual. If you have got someone who can swing in a decent corner against Gretna you do not need hardly anybody else and I got 2 assists and hit the bar from 20 yds and in the changing room everybody was clapping me on the back and a fella called Duffy who is the captain told me I woud probily get the league player of the month award on the basis of just that 1 game. Well I dident want say anything Joe as I dont want to look big headed but I guess they dont see many performances like that in this league and altho I have missed the other 2 matches this month you coud say that I have made up for it with that 1.

It is funny how quickly you get used to some things Joe like training kit with your initials on it or having your own squad number but I guess all that just distracts you from the real busness at hand and that is winning games and EK was already 6 points clear of the league when I arrived and it is prity good money I will drag them over the finishing line so to speak. Of coarse if they win the lowland league they will maybe get up into the 4th division same as East Fife and I woud not be able to stay with them Joe as I need to be on at lease the same amount of money as I am right now but I guess you never know how much cash there is sloshing around in the $4^{th}$ division and a good young player is reely more of an investment than a layout Joe and if EK sold me on for say £500k at the end of next season that woud still be a good return on theys money. But I have always been 1 for seeing a little further ahead than other people and I guess I shoud focus on the short term for now and see abt winning our next game against Cumbernauld.

Your pal,

Andy


February 2nd

Well Joe I only mentioned it to you in passing just to let you know how highly I am thought of here but I got the phone call threw this morning and it turns out I have won the league player of the month award after all even tho I only played 1 match in January. I did not even know that the lowland league had a player of the month award which I guess shows you how far out of the picture Selkirk are but apparently they is a big awards ceremony at Hampden tomorrow evening. If that shot against Gretna had been ½ an inch lower they coud have saved themselfs some bother and come round to my house with the goal of the month award too but you shoud not look a gift horse in the mouth as they say and an award like this can only serve me well in the long term.

Of coarse nobody from my old club has been in touch to congratulate me which is funny as usually I cannot leave the fridge door open without old Donaldson phones me and says what the hell are you doing. I guess they must be phoning around all the van hire companies looking for the cheapest quote to get all of there awards back from the ceremony tomorrow and I am joking of coarse Joe but I wish they was at lease a flop of the month award so that 1 of them woud be their to see me get some recognition from my peers.

I will need to buy a suit Joe as I dont have 1 and I dont know much abt award ceremonys but I dont think I can just turn up in jeans and a pac man t shirt. I will need to look my best as I expect their will be tv cameras and probily women too and if the ladys football teams have their awards nites at the same time all the better Joe eh. I will pop in to TK Max tomorrow morning and see what suits they have got and I woud like something in gray or pale blue but I will probily just get the cheapest 1 that is in my size or at least within a size or 2 and I dont know if they is a cash prize to go with the award but sints I stopped getting any appearance money from the club I have been struggling to make ends meet. But I guess someone at this stage in their career reely ought to have a suit as you never know when you will need to look your best and if I am going to be at EK until the end of the season that is five more player of the month awards I will be picking up and I am only jokeing of coarse Joe but it is a joke that has some truth in it as somebody would have to reely go some and play out of there skins if they wanted to finish ahead of me in the awards race.

Well Joe I do not supose the ceremony will be live on the tv and even if it was you probily woudent be able to get it in Selkirk because they will be too busy showing a programme abt the oldest post box in Melrose but I will send you a link to the awards ceremony when I get it and it will be strange for you eh Joe seeing your old pal Andy rubbing shoulders with all these famous people but I hope you dont think it will make any diffrents between me and you Joe as in the future it will be hard for me to make new friends on acct I wont know if they just like me because I am famous but I will always know that my old pal Joe was looking out for me even way back when I lived in a one horse burg like Selkirk and you will always be the 1$^{st}$ name on my list at dinner partys Joe although I woud probily have to set you at a different table from the famous people as they might find it a bit weird otherwise.

Your pal,

Andy


February 4th


Well Joe I turned up at Hampden last nite just for a laugh and of coarse their was no one their just like I expected and it is funny how locked up tight the place is in the evening Joe and it was only 7pm so you woud think someone from the SFA woud still have been in their racking there branes abt how to get Scottish football back on track but their was not a single light on in the whole place which I guess is why this country is such a fix.

The truth is Joe that I only went along because I thought the EK lads woud be waiting for me with a pretend award or something and I dident want to disapoint them only they were not and the pretend award was sitting in my space when I went into the changing room this pm and it was a KFC bucket with glitter and PVA glue and my name written on it in black marker. Well they was all watching to see what I woud do Joe but I dident want to give them the satisfaction so I picked it up and then kissed it and held it up like it was the world cup and they all laughed and clapped their hands and started chanting speech speech speech and I cleared my throte and said that altho it was always nice to be singled out I was here standing in for the whole team just like I do every Satterday and everybody bust out laughing and Duffy clapped me on the back and said that it was a team ritual and they needed to have some way of seeing what kind of fella they were bringing on board whenever a new player came to the club but that I had showed everyone I was a good egg as well as a good football player and they was glad to have me with them and I said well it is nice to be here and I appresiate the amount of effort that has went in to this award and it showed a lot of imagination for you guys to think of a player of the month award when you has probily only read abt them in the newspapers. So everything come off alright in the end Joe although I am still £50 out for a suit that I will not need until the next time I win an award altho that maybe wont be as far away as people think.

Only thing is Joe I invited that girl I told you abt from my collage coarse to come along to the awards ceremony and she texted strait back saying she woud love to and I texted her back saying that it was a big deal to win the award after only 1 game for East Kilbride and her phone must of run out of battery after that Joe as she never texted back altho it is just as well sints she woud probily not have seen the joke and the stairs at Hampden Park must be reely difficult to walk up in high heals which is maybe why they are always saying their is not enough women in Scottish football. But I hope she does not think I snubbed her Joe or found someone better to go with and I will tell her that at collage on Tuesday but I cant see any reason why she woud not have got back to me exept maybe that her battery run out.

Your pal,

Andy

February 12th


Well Joe it is only 8 months or so sints I played in the Lowland League for Selkirk but it does not take too long to get used to how the other half live. I have got used to the way things are off the field as I am not no Billy big time that thinks he is too good to clean his own boots and anyway I had to clean my own boots at my other club so that woud not make no diffrents either way but what I am getting at is that the football is very diffrent in the Lowland League and in most ways it is a lot easier and the players at this level are so basic that winning against them is like taking candy from a baby. The thing is Joe that altho there is a physical side to the teams in the top division and some of the guys up there are built like tanks all and all it is only part of the game where as in the Lowland League the physical side is the entire game and every team has got 10-11 players who are no good at anything but shoulder charging and standing on your feet.

Sints I have been running my legs off and living on

starvation rations at my old club Joe the weight has dropped right off and before I went up to the big time there was no one in the Lowland League had an extra lb on me but now there are teamfuls of 16 yr olds jakies who coud smash rite thro me like I am a crisp packet in the wind. So I am having to get a lot better at dodging out the way Joe which is a useful skill to have but their is a reason why in WWI they gave the troops that were going over the top guns Joe and did not just teach them how to dodge really quick.

We have made it 3 wins out of 3 so far Joe and the confidents has been oozing threw the side. I have been doing my sums to work out how many more points we need only the calculater on my phone is wonky and it keeps coming up with diffrent answers so we either need 15 or 22 depending but I shoud not worry abt that Joe because as long as we keep takeing it 1 game at a time and getting the 3 points we will win the league at a canter altho it might be a bit closer if it is 22 points we need instead of 15. We are away to Whitehill Welfare this weekend and I dont remember them being any grate sheiks and you will remember better than anyone

Joe that they dont even have a stand they just have some steps in front of there pavilion for people to sit on and the reason I say that you know that better than anyone is because you have spent so much time sitting on those steps that one of them has got a plack on it dedicated to you. I am only jokeing of coarse Joe but I do remember you spending a lot of time watching games instead of playing them and it takes a lot of patients to put up with being overlooked time and time again and I take my hat off to you Joe for sticking on in their when most people woud of realised it was never going to work out in 1 million years.

But I thought I woud mention it to you anyway Joe as Whitehill Welfare is only less than 1 hour away from you and you will probily not be playing on Saturday so I thought you might want to come up and sit on those steps agane for old times sake and see your old pal Andy playing for the league leaders and nabbing another 3 points for EK. I scored a free kick right in the postage stamp last Satterday agenst Dalbeattie Star and old Mackinnon has said if I keep it up he will be putting me on penaltys too and it is a shame my goal bonus only counts for goals I score for my other club as if I was getting paid by the goal here I woud be on to a prity good deal Joe tho I have only scored 1 so far but that is because I am busy laying them on for other people and I coud score any time I get on the ball if I wanted to.

Anyway Joe let me know abt you comeing to the Whitehill game as it woud be good to see my old pal again altho I coudent only speak to you for maybe five minutes afterwards as I have to sit with the EK players when we eat and it woud look a bit weird if you came and sat with us and people woud probily think you were some kind of joker who is trying to nab a free meal and I woud not mind for myself Joe only it is you I am thinking of.

Your pal,

Andy


February 14th

Well Joe it is probily for the best that you are not able to make it to the Whitehill game altho I think you are being a bit optimistic that you are going to be in the Selkirk squad this weekend even if ½ the team are away on a stag do but I woud not want to reign on your parade and stranger things have happened as they say and their is no harm in hoping for the best so long as you do not get upset when it doesent happen as it is a bit embarrassing for everybody else when someone causes a big scene like that.

Anyway Joe I am feeling a bit under the wether lately what with this and that and I have a feeling that I wont be fit for the game and will not play. I have been feeling like this for a wile now Joe and I guess that woud explane why I have only got 1 goal in 3 games played and probily a rest woud be the best thing for me right now. It is hard to put my finger on it but if I had to describe it I woud say I am feeling prity run down and not reely fit to travel ½ the way across the country for a game we are going to win anyway and I have played every minute of every game so far Joe which of coarse is on merit but old Mackinnon doesent seem to have herd of such a thing as squad management and if things keep going the way they are I will wind up burning out before this season is over. I know I use to play week in week out for Selkirk but I am not just talking abt the physical strain Joe I am talking abt the mental strain and there is not reely much of that at Selkirk where you are expected to get beat 99 times out of 100 but at EK you are expected to win every game which is a lot to cope with especially when you are the clubs biggest signing ever and that is a lot of pressure to put on anyone Joe without telling them that the player they will be up against in the next game is an actual psychopath which is what old Duffy told me this pm.

I was getting my boots on in the changeing room and just minding my own busness Joe like I think everybody shoud do when old Duffy tramps along and stands their watching me and finely he says your not going to ware those on Satterday are you and I says no these are just my boots for training so he says good because you woud be as well wareing a pair of slippers as those things as far as protection goes and you are going to need all the protection you can get against

Crusher McGrew and I says who the hell is Crusher McGrew when he is at home and Duffy says well nobody on acct he is never at home unless he has got a timeshare on an isolation cell up in Barlinnie but I guess I shoud not have said anything abt it as when Crusher McGrew takes against someone there is no boots on earth that is going to save him exept maybe some running shoes and I said well there is no danger of his taking agenst me as I never even heard of him before. Well old Duffy laughed at that and he said then I guess you have not watched any MMA fighting lately although I supose he has not been on the tv much sints that bloodbath agenst Williams but as for why he has got a problem with you well apparently you have been going around badmouthing Methel a lot lately and that is Crushers home town.

Well Joe I dident say anything for a wile after that and then Duffy patted me on the shoulder and said obviously I know you were only jokeing abt Methel but Crusher is not libel to see things that way and it is going to be a prity dicey afternoon for you so we will do our best to tip you a nod if it looks like he is abt to fly off in to 1 of his rages. The only problem is you will be marking him at corners and in the mist of the confusion anything coud happen and all you can do is try to stay in plane site of the referee so that if McGrew does anything at lease he will get sent off as well and that way your sacrifice will not have been in vain.

Well Joe I dont know who has spread the word that I have been saying bad things abt Methel and I was only saying it tongue in cheek as it were and if I had the chance I woud explane that to Crusher and I am sure he woud understand but it does not look like I will be fit in time for the game anyway and if I am not playing I woud be better off resting up in bed rather than going on a wide goose chase to Whitehill just to sit on the steps like a reject so I guess old Crusher will go to his grave thinking that I said bad things abt his home town. The whole thing goes to show you Joe that you shoud not believe every little thing you here as I am sure I woud be able to explane to Crusher that it was all just a mistake and that someone who comes from Selkirk has got no busness running any bodys home town in to the ground but I guess I wont get the chance now on acct of whatever it is that is wrong with me.

Your pal,

Andy


February 16th


Well Joe when I woke up this morning I coud hardly
get out of bed so I called old Mackinnon to let him
know that I wasent up to playing and he said that is fine
but I guess you are fit enough to get on a bus and come
watch and I said well yes but I am not well and there is
nobody else in the team comes to watch the games
when they are ill and Mackinnon said there is nobody
else in the team that is on full time wages and Barry
Donaldson sent you here on the condition that we did
not go easy on you and I am going to stick to that. So
there you go Joe it seems like I am never going to shake
off old Donaldson and his bony clutches and even
from beyond the grave he is working his magic on me
so to speak. So I had to get my stuff on and and get in

to East Kilbride in time to catch the team bus and I was running late on acct of how poorly I felt and every one gived a big cheer when I finely got on the bus and old Mackinnon said to the driver well that is the bullion on board so I guess we can make a start.

Well Joe we had hardly got out of East Kilbride before old Mackinnon was sitting down next to me and saying I am glad to see you going above and beyond for the sake of the team Andy only whatever it is that is wrong with you there seems to be a lot of it going around and the squad is down the the bear bones so woud you be ok if I named you on the bench just in case and so I said yes as there is no point in going all that way just to sit on the stairs Joe and at lease this way I woud get to be on the bench away from all the old men that was always asking you why you were not aloud to play and kind of makeing fun of you a bit. Well Joe you give these people an inch and they take a mile and next thing I knew old Mackinnon had me saying I woud play from the start and I guess sometimes Joe there is no escaping your fate and you have just got to put up with things the best you can even when you have got a raging fever and you feel like your bones are made out of wet toilet paper.

Well Crusher McGrew was not a real big guy like I expected Joe and in fact he was kind of on the scrawny side but I guess most of these kinds of people are when you think abt it Joe as when did you ever see a fat serial killer. But I wasent takeing any chances Joe and whenever he got within abt 5 ft of me I passed the ball away strait away and I was worried that he might be getting more and more enraged every time I did it Joe and he might wind up doing something desprit but he did not let it discourage him and he just kept comeing at me and comeing at me but never getting anywhere close and at corners I just did what I always do which is to keep my distants Joe so that they cannot duck onto my blind side and get the jump on me and in the end Joe we run out 5-0 winners and I did not get no goals or assists but I did not see no point in antagonising old Crusher any more than I had to and after the game Crusher shook my hand nice as pie which I guess shows that he realises that someone as good at football as I am is a worthy opponent and woud never say anything bad abt someones home town and old Mackinnon said in the changeing room that it was good to see me not clinging on to the ball like it was a life belt for a change and that it was my quick cycling of possession that was the key to our victry and I said well what do you expect when you have got a psychopath like McGrew breatheing down your neck and everybody else laughed and old Duffy slipped me the wink as if to say well done for stepping up to the plate and acting with grace under pressure when the team needed me most and without me they woud have been up against it big time and it was only a wink Joe but sometimes you can say quite a lot without words.

I have checked to see if the Lowland League does a player of the month award Joe sints it is getting to the end of February but I cannot find no menshun of it which I guess makes sents as from what I have seen so far it woud be like giveing out actual gold medals at a school sports day.

Your pal,

Andy

February 22nd


Well Joe finely some good has come of all those
performances I have been turning in over the last few
weeks and old Mackinnon took me to 1 side today and
told me he wants me takeing all our free kicks and
penaltys from now on. I guess you woud think that is
no big deal Joe as I am not on any goal bonus or
anything but their are so many fouls in this league that I
coud easy get a hat trick every game off the back of
penaltys and free kicks and the way I see it Joe the more
goals I can put beside my name at the end of the season
the more chance their is of me being picked up by
someone and it is beginning to look like I will need to
find a club for next year Joe as old Mackinnon was kind
of hinting that I will not be able to stay on at EK. He
asked me what my plans were for next season and I
told him I did not have any but that I coud always fall
back on EK if nothing else better came along and
Mackinnon laughed and said that was good to know but

that someone with my level of ability shoud not be thinking abt playing for East Kilbride but shoud be looking to get themselfs back in to the professional game. He said that his job was not to keep me at EK but to help me get back to the level I belonged and that he coud help me do that if I kept on listening to him and doing what he asked. Well Joe it is the 1$^{st}$ I have heard that I am listening to him and doing what he asks and it is not hard to follow someones instructions when all they ever say is keep it nice and simple today lads and lets get these 3 points on the board. But he is a nice guy Joe and I am sure he woud bite my hand off to have me playing for EK next season and he is probily just hard balling me on wages etc when he comes off with all that stuff abt looking for another club. I have picked up a thing or 2 abt busness over the last few months you see Joe and maybe the best thing old Donaldson ever did for my career was send to me collage and the 2$^{nd}$ best thing was sending me to EK. It was a good thing I got out when I did Joe and I dont know if you have been following there results and I woudent bother exept that I set up the alerts on my phone and I dont know how to turn them off but they have totally went off the rails sints they sent me out on lone and if it wasent for that lucky win against Kilmarnock last week they woud only have got 2 wins sints new year.

The days are a lot longer now that I have training in the pm instead of the am Joe and of coarse they woud be longer still if I dident have collage to go to and I guess some players have got familys to go home to Joe but a lot of them seem to be at a loose end like myself and when I use to ask what everybody was doing after training back at the old club most everybody was off to the races or whatever and even at EK where nobody has got hardly any cash to lose everybody is always talking abt how much they made on this bet or that bet at the weekend tho if you want a gamble that is as safe as houses Joe it is that nobody will ever mention it if their bet dident come in.

But listen Joe if you wanted to pick up a bit of money on the side and I have never known you not to it woud not be a bad idea for you to bet on yrs truly for 1st goalscorer in the game against Preston Atletic this Satterday as they are a proper bunch of cloggers and if they dont give us at least a penalty or 2 I will eat my hat and if I am 12 yards out from the goalkeeper you know I will make sure of it. Of coarse it will depend on whether 1 of the poachers who play up front for us get in their before Preston have the chance to foul anybody but their is no chance at all of Preston getting the 1$^{st}$ goal or any of the goals after that so it is probily quite a bit better than even money Joe and seeing as I am 10 to 1 to score the 1$^{st}$ goal so you dont need no busness degree from collage to tell that it is money in the bank.

Your pal,

Andy


February 25th


Well Joe I am at my wits end and I dont know whether I am comeing or going and what shoud have been the best day of my life has turned out to be 1 of the worse and their is only 1 person who can get me out of this whole jam and it is my good pal Joe who I have always relied on and tried to do a good turn for whenever I can and it is not much that I am asking you Joe and I never asked you for nothing before but you can see this is reely important and I am at the end of my rope so I will tell you what has happent and I only hope you can help me Joe as otherwise I am reely up against it this time for sure.

Well Joe I know that the 1st result you will have been looking out for on Satterday was East Kilbride now that your old pal is plying his trade their so to speak and of coarse if you were watching the updates on sky sports news you will have wondered what was going on at Preston and you wont be suprised to here that what was going on at Preston was your old pal Andy. I got 2 goals in the 1st half Joe and 1 was a penalty and 1 was a total raker and I got another penalty right at the end of the game for 3 goals all together Joe which is a hat trick and when you add in the other 4 goals we scored I woud say that I got assists on most of them and you will see Joe that it was a bit of a one man band against Preston and you dont often get performances like that in the modern age in my opinion.

Well I got plenty of plaudits after the game Joe and everyone wanted a peace of me and the guy from the East Lothian Currier or something had me talking for ¼ of an hour so by the time I got changed and got back to the bus everyone and his dog was making jokes abt what a superstar I am and how somebody from a big club shoud come and have a look at me as I woud be sure to be a smash hit in the big leagues etc. Well Joe I was takeing it all in my stride as I always do when Duffy sat down next to me in the bus and he had a paper plate from the clubroom and he sat there munching his queesh and raveing abt the performance I just put in and then finely he said well I am sure glad to have you on board with us Andy even if its murder on the bus axels and its just a shame you cant bet on yourself to finish top scorer in the league or you woud make a tidy sum. So I said to him well why cant I bet on myself and he said well for 1 thing proffeshunal footballers is not aloud to bet on profeshunal football which of coarse doesent reely effect us as we are all only amatures exept you but for another thing if we were to bet on something that we have got control over it woud be unfair and a big no no like we coud bet on you to be 1$^{st}$

goalscorer and then make sure you score the 1$^{st}$ goal. So I dident say anything for a wile after that and then I told Duffy that just because you are doing everything you can to help me score a goal doesent mean I will and Duffy nodded and said yes youre telling me but the point is if you have a conversation with someone abt something you think might happen in a game you are playing in and then that person bets money on it and wins then it is going to look very fishy to the authorities who are enclined to take a dim view of such things but I dont know why you are getting your knickers in a twist because unless some poor sap has bet good money on you to score today there is not no problem and unless they have put a Ladbrokes in the loony bin there is no chance that anybody bet you to score today. And then Duffy started back on his queesh like he was in love with it and I just looked out the window the rest of the way home.

So you can see Joe the bind that I am in and I guess you realise that I was only jokeing when I said before abt how you shoud bet on me as 1$^{st}$ goalscorer as obviously there is no guarantee that I was going to score the 1<sup>st</sup> goal and it was just a good bet that anyone coud have seen and taken advantage of whether they know me or not so if anyone from the police or the SFA asks you abt it Joe I hope you will tell them the truth and just say that you know how good a player I am and that the odds they had me on to score were crazy and any gambler worth his salt woud have jumped on them and if you just tell them that Joe and dont mention our little joke abt the bet it woud be a lot better if you see what I am getting at. I know that I can count on you Joe and I will owe you 1 in the future and if you ever needed me to alibi you for the police Joe you know I woud do it in a heartbeat and the time I told Mrs Craig that it was you who threw the rubber it was only because it was in chemistry and it coud have been dangerous but otherwise I woud always alibi for you Joe and I hope you know that.

Your pal,

Andy


February 27th

I got your message Joe and thanks for letting me know that you did not bet on me to score as that gets us both off the hook big time Joe altho I can not help wondering why you did not put any money on it and it seems to me that most people woud probily have faith in their old pal who they have seen 1st hand become 1 of the most highly rated midfeilders in East Kilbride and it is not as if you are short of money Joe on acct your parents dont even charge you digs and if I had been put on to a tip like that by someone who I trusted I woud have thought it was good for £5 pounds at lease. But I supose it is your own look out what you do with your money Joe and obviously I am glad that you did not bet anything in this case as it woud have looked a bit funny someone who coud not pick a winner in a race between a jackrabbit and a jumping bean suddenly hitting the jackpot out of nowhere and so I am glad you dident Joe even tho it doesent make any sense to me.

Your pal,

Andy

March 2nd


Well Joe we have not dropped a single point sints I arrived and that is including against all the teams in the top 4 exept for the team at the top of the table which is ourselfs but we have also been professhunal enough to do the job against the little teams as well even though playing against us is kind of like a cup final for them and you can see them raise there game or try to anyway. I guess it must be a real thrill for the shelf stackers at Gala Fairydean to be on the same pitch as a professhunal like myself and I supose 1 or 2 of them think that if they turn on a good performance against me then someone from my other club will set up and take notice but the truth is Joe that if someone was to pull out a gun and shoot me on the pitch in Gala probily old Donaldson woudent have nothing to say abt it exept maybe Andy who tho of coarse there is no chance of anybody in Gala pulling out a gun and shooting me or anything else that takes a bit of initiative and if theys hole house was on fire they woudent think to open the windows unless someone from the council told them to.

Well Joe I coud care less what someone from Gala thinks of me as we are not even playing their until April but the fixture list has thrown up a real cracker this weekend and I woud not even have noticed it if Duffy had not asked me yesterday if I was thinking abt getting my haircut one of these days and I said what do you mean and he said well I thought you might want to look your best for the hail the conkering hero parade when we go down to Selkirk this Satterday. Well of coarse Joe I thought he was jokeing as I had forgot that Selkirk were in the same league as us but he showed me the fixture list in the match program and their it was in black and white Selkirk vs East Kilbride. I guess you will have had that fixture circled for weeks Joe but I honestly had not given it a thought.

So Duffy was makeing all these cracks abt how everyone back home will be looking forward to seeing me and it must not be every day that someone new comes to Selkirk and especially not if they have been once before but the truth is Joe what with 1 thing and another I never mentioned to anyone in Selkirk that I had been loned out to East Kilbride and even my mum and dad have somehow got it into there heads that the reason I am not playing for my other team these days is because I am enjured. So it will probily come as a bit of a suprise to them when I roll back in to town on Satterday with a bunch of guys who have to wash there own training kit.

It is not that I am embarrassed or anything like that Joe as playing for East Kilbride is still a cut above anything that anybody else from Selkirk has managed but some people dont reely like suprises and I dont think it is fare to spring 1 on them like that plus whenever you tell people 1 thing and then they get the wrong end of the stick and think you said something else they are libel to believe that you lied to them on purpose and of coarse Joe I have never lied to anyone exept maybe by not telling them the whole storey and if anyone thinks otherwise you will be able to vouch for me as I never told you anything but the truth even when you dident want to here it.

So what I was thinking Joe is that maybe you coud sort of lay the ground work so to speak by hinting to the rest of the team that there is a big suprise comeing for them on Satterday and that it is something which has been planned for months and that way when I turn up on Satterday people will think the reason that I dident tell them abt joining East Kilbride was so that I coud play this prank on them by just showing up and of coarse that is a lot closer to the truth than anything else they might think Joe and I have always been a bit of a practical joke as they say so it woud all tie in prity good. Only you will need to let them know by sort of hinting that something is abt to come off Joe and that will mean that you will have to axshully speak to someone for a change instead of just sitting their in the corner and I guess the big surprise for the guys in the changing room will be that you are not a deaf mute after all and my playing for East Kilbride will be a distant 2$^{nd}$. Of coarse Joe if you just spoke to someone every once in a wile I guess everyone at Selkirk woud already know that I was playing for East Kilbride and the reason I tell you everything that is going on with me is so that you can pass it on Joe as I do not have time to get in touch with every single last person and let them know what flavour of cup a soup I had that morning. But it is all by the by now Joe and all I am saying is that you do not do yourself any favours with that attitude.

So Joe I will probily see you on Satterday as I expect you will still be at the game even if you are not in the squad just to see your old pal Andy and if you coud remember to let people know abt the prank I have been playing on them these last few weeks I woud appresiate it.

Your pal,

Andy


March 5th


Well Joe I looked for you all over on Satterday but I coud not find you any place and I even tried looking on the Selkirk bench but nobody had seen you their in weeks. I guess you might have been their Joe and thought you coudent come up and say hello now that I am a professhunal footballer but I have always treated you the same Joe irregardless of which 1 of us is the professhunal and I hope you did not think I am too fancy for my old pal Joe now especially seeing as nobody else seems to think that and if I had a penny for every time someone clapped me on the back on Satterday and said well well the wanderer returns I woud be able to live off the interest for years.

I dont know if you were there or not Joe and I supose you wasnt as it was not exactly a bumper crowd and I guess you have finely got to a place where you dont show up if you are not playing which by now probily means you have forgotten where Yarrow Park is and I am glad you have finely got some self respect Joe but it woud have been nice if you had turned out for your old pal Andy is all I am saying as I doubt you will see me playing at Yarrow Park again any time soon.

Anyway Joe I dont know if you got the chance to spread the word abt our little prank but when I got to Selkirk everyone was expecting me and was reely glad to see me so you might have overdone it a little with the hinting and to be honest it woud have been nice if people had been at lease a little bit suprised instead of acting as if it was the most natral thing in the world for me to playing for East Kilbride but it is a fine line you are treding with these jokes and it was nice to see that everyone was happy for me and remembered everything I had done for the club and of coarse for all they know I have been sent to EK to get match experience rather than because I faced down old Donaldson and made him quake in his boots so to speak.

Anyway Joe it woud have been good to see you and to be honest if old Fergie was any kind of sport he woud have given you a game as he woud have known that it woud not make no earthly difrents and the only way things woud have turned out diffrently woud have been if I felt sorry for my old pal Joe and took my foot off the gas a little bit instead of batting him around like a cat with a ball of wool but in the end it was 4-0 going on 10 and I coud have got a hat trick if I had wanted but I kept myself down to 1 and after I scored it I only celebrated a little bit out of respect to my old team. I guess it was not the 1st time that the only thing keeping Selkirk from an absolute scalding was me Joe but I hope it will be the last.

The chareman showed me around the club before the game and I went around with him just to be polite but of coarse nothing much has changed and even the biscuit under the pool table is still their so it shows you they have not exactly raised their game sints I left. I dont know who the lad was that was playing in midfeild instead of me and of coarse he has big shoes to fill but he was no Frantz Beckonbower Joe and if I was not able to get in the team ahead of him I woud put my heavy boots on and walk into the sea tho that is no reflection on you Joe as I know you get a bum rap from managers on acct of you being such a small guy. But what I am saying Joe is that you have got to keep moveing forward as a club and if you stand still nowadays you get left behind and it was only 12 months ago that scouts from the biggest clubs in the country was making a b line for Yarrow Park and now it woud take a zombie apocalypse to get anybody there who is not playing for Selkirk.

I guess the old saying is true Joe that you dont know what you have got until you have lost it and there were a couple more cracks abt my size than was necesary but it was funny to be sitting their in the same old club room after the game with the same old chicken curry in the same old paper plates and the only diffrents was that I was sitting on the other side of the room with the away players and it dident feel quite right Joe. I guess in some ways Joe I do miss the old place and it woud nice to be able to come back here for a season before I retire but for that Selkirk will need to get promoted to at lease the 3$^{rd}$ division as their is no way I am dropping down to the hobo leagues again.

The chareman must have been thinking the same thing Joe because when I went up to get a coke he asked me when I woud be comeing back to sign for Selkirk and I said maybe sooner than you think and he laughed and said well dont make it too soon son as we are brakeing even on the kitchen sints you left and we have got 10% of your next transfer fee comeing so if you sign for Real Madrid we might even be able to clear our tab with the cash and carry and then he paid for my drink Joe which I supose he thinks makes us even for the money he owes me but even at Selkirk the coke does not cost £100 pounds tho I guess if he thought he coud get away with it he woud do it the old cheap skate.

Anyway Joe I was sorry not to see you their but I will be back some time in the future and If I can swing it with whatever team I play for next season to come down to Selkirk for a friendly some time I definately will as long as it is written into the contract that my old pal Joe has to play as well.

Your pal,

Andy


March 7th


Well Joe as you know I am someone that you have to get up prity early in the am if you want to put 1 over on them and the deeper into things that you get the more you see that people are lineing up round the block to make you look like an idiot and so when the boys around the club were talking abt my winning the player of the month award for February today I took it all with a pinch of salt as they say. I dont mind takeing 1 on the chin for team moral every once in a wile Joe but 1$^{st}$ and fourmost I am here to play football not to take a custard pie in the face whenever someone is feeling a bit down on themselfs. So when everyone was comeing up to me in the changeing room and shakeing my hand and telling me how much I deserved it I kept my face totally strait Joe like I always do and did not give no reaction 1 way or another but just got on with rapping the tape around my ankels and being a proffeshunal.

So after a bit Duffy comes over and says well I am glad to see that you are exited abt the news but I wish you woud calm down a bit as you are starting to put everyone else on edge. It is not every day that someone wins player of the month around here but you are kind of acting like it is. So anyway Joe I still dident say anything and Duffy was abt to take off when he stopped and laughed and said ok Andy you got us this time and I guess the joke is on us and I only wish you was as quick to get wise when it came to Cumbernaulds set piece routines as you were to catch on to us. Well Joe everybody started laughing and Duffy said look we had even set up a little fake news website to trick you and he showed me it on his phone Joe and it looked prity real but I did not read it proper as I did not want Duffy to think I was getting sucked in as these guys are like sharks when it comes to reeling you in and if they think they have got a bite they are totally ruthless. So I put my boots on and said well I am sorry to ruin your fun this time boys but you know what they say once bitten twice shy and I walked out the changeing room door only their was a man with a big camera their and as soon as I opened the door everybody started cheering all at once and there was another man who handed me a trophy and said congratulations and how does it feel and to be honest with you Joe even then I thought it might still be a prank exept I coud see old Mackinnon standing with his arms folded and he is not someone who is libel to accept that kind of monkeying around so I tried to answer the mans questions Joe but I coud not think what to say and they had to let me have a moment to myself before they took me off some place quieter and asked me again and I dont know if anyone will ever ask you abt your playing career Joe but it is not easy to come up with things to say and so you wind up talking abt how grate your teammates are and how the award is reely for them even tho that is not true at all Joe and if they were so grate they woud of been standing their instead of you. But that is not what you are ment to say Joe and I am a proffeshunal so I talked all abt my teammates even tho it was me that did the lions share of the work.

Well after the interview was finished and the tv men drove away old Mackinnon came up and said well done and I had handled it very well and the trophy was a just reward for all the hard work I had put in at the club. Well the trophy looked like it had cost 50p in a Poundland discount sale and you coud not tell if the figure on it was playing football or darts but I knew what he meant Joe and what he was trying to say was that I am single handedly dragging this team towards the finish line and without me they woud not have no chance and if there was some recognition comeing my way because of that it was only fair. Only he did not say it in so many words Joe because old Mackinnon is a proffeshunal like myself in spite of his beard and he knows that it is bad for team moral for 1 player to get all the attention even if they are the best player by a country mile. And then old Mackinnon said well you have missed the 1st half of training so you will need to get out there and work all the harder to catch up and I woud not get too attached to that wee trophy of yours because their will be plenty more where that came from if you just keep sticking in and doing what your manager asks of you. So just to butter him up a bit Joe I said that I woud always listen to him and do whatever he wanted and he laughed and said that was good to know but that he woud not always be my manager and that if I kept on playing the way I was he woud not be suprised if I turned a head or 2 even before the end of the season.

Well Joe I guess I shoud have been on top of the world after my big success but for some reason I felt a little sad after talking to old Mackinnon and even after training with all the boys and they were all so pleased for me and acting as if I had won the world cup or something but it is only a cheap little trophy that dont mean anything in the grand scheme of things and I guess I shoud feel as if everything has come up trumps Joe but I dont and if anything I feel like the bottom has fallen out of the world but I am dammed if I coud tell you why.

Your pal,

Andy


March 10th


You know how when a player moves on from a club Joe he does a big story abt how the team will always have a special place in his heart and they will be the 1st result he looks out for on a Satterday. Well Joe I can tell you from my direct experience that that is a load of hooey and once a player has cleared his towels out his locker the whole club might as well stop existing for all he is concerned and I dont blame him Joe because quite apart from anything once a club thinks they have got you caring abt them that is that and they will pay you as little as they think they can get away with and I have herd storys abt guys who got a tattoo of theys club logo 1 week and were on ½ their old wages the next because that is where sentiment gets you in this game Joe you can take it from me.

I have not been paying much attention to what has been going on at my old club sints I left Joe as it has got 0 to do with me and as long as the pay checks keep on comeing in the whole place coud go on fire tomorow and I woud not think twice abt it. But the newspapers are making such a big song and dance over old Donaldson that I am seeing his stupid face everywhere I look right now no matter how hard I try to avoid it. Well Joe he might have won a manager of the month award but all that means is he had a load of easy games that month and it is just the luck of the draw Joe and everybody will get a few weeks like that at some point so they might as well divvy out the manager of the month awards at the start of the season for all the diffrents it woud make. It makes me laugh to see the newspapers touting him as the next big thing in

Scottish management when he has got no ideas abt motivation or anything like that and you can have all the talent in the world Joe but it is no use to you if you do not know how to deal with people.

What is even funnier Joe is they are all saying what a great season he is haveing even tho the club has suposedly been hit by enjuries but that does not make no sents to me Joe as he is responsible for putting the squad together and if the players he has signed are not up to the job then that is surely on him and if you sign a busful of old has beens that is held together by snot and blu tak why shoud you get any credit for it. I guess he coud take the club all the way down to the 4$^{th}$ division and still be getting all the plaudits so long as he had more players in the GPs office than on the pitch.

I guess it sounds like I am prity bitter Joe and most people woud think I have every right to be when old Donaldson is in the newspapers every week getting sympathy for all his enjured players when the 1 fit player he has got is out here at East Kilbride running laps round Strathclyde Park and if I am not totaled yet Joe it is not for want of his trying. But that it how it is in this busness Joe it is a dog eat dog world and you have got to be the dog that is eating the other dog not the dog that is being eaten.

Your pal,

Andy


March 13th


Well Joe another week another win and we are only 2 wins away from rapping up the title. We woud have done it by the end of the month exept we have got that cup match agenst Berwick Rangers next week which it seems is quite a big deal for everyone at EK and 1 of the biggest games in the clubs history and I am looking forward to it mainly to see the looks on their faces when we arrive at the Berwick stadium and everyone finds out it is not the San Siro they think it is but more like the inside of an old Matchbox car someone dug out a sandpit.

Today was just candy from a baby Joe and I scored a free kick and got an assist from another free kick and in the changeing rooms afterwards everybody was saying that we will rap up the league at Gala Fairydean next month if everything goes according to plan which woud be a dream come true for me Joe as I will not get many more opportunities to stick 1 to the Fairydean once I am back in the big leagues so I will definitely make the most of it and I will enjoy getting it right up there wee fat groundskeeper as why woud you have a groundskeeper when your pitch is made of astroturf Joe it doesent make any sents.

But old Mackinnon came in and stopped us from getting too carried away and he said that we have got a big cup game to focus on 1$^{st}$ and it will be a real feather in our caps if we can get a result against Berwick and hopefully move on to a big money spinner in the next round and it woud make people sit up and take notice of the club that we are putting together down here. Then he asked me outside for a quick word and he told me that it probily wasent what I wanted to hear but he dident know if I woud be able to play against Berwick on acct that you are only aloud to play for 1 team in the cup per season and my main club might not want me cup tied to playing for EK. But my 3 month loan is up on Monday and Mackinnon has to speak to old Donaldson abt terms for extending it anyway so he is going to see abt twisting the old mans arm into letting me play.

Well it woud be just like old Donaldson to stop me from being involved in 1 of the clubs biggest ever games just out of spite Joe and it is not so much for myself Joe as it means 0 to me to play against Berwick Rangers but the club is going to need all the help it can get and if they coud win this game we woud be in the next round with the big guns and it is 0 to me Joe who has already played in Europe but it woud make a lot of people around here very proud to see their boys mixing it up with the crem della crem and the dinner lady had tears running down her face when we beat Civil Service Strollers so you can imagine how it will be if we knock out Berwick Rangers.

Your pal,

Andy


March 15th


Joe

They have turned down my lone extension. I am to report back to training tomorrow.

Your pal,

Andy

# The Magic of the Cup

March 16th

Well Joe I had kind of got used to training in the pm as there is no point dragging people up out their beds when they are ½ asleep but if you have training in the pm the players get there morning to thereselfs and you have something to look forward to as you have run out of things to do by abt 1pm and training does not seem like such a chore by then. But when it is 8am and you are leaning over the sink with your toothbrush in your hand and the 1st thing you are doing as soon as you wake up is shuttle runs it is hard to believe that this is what your life has come to.

As well as that Joe training in the pm means players can have other jobs if they like and wile I was at EK I coud have got a couple of shifts at the Tesco or whatever and made myself a bit of extra £ but I dident think of that so I just stayed at home buying things off the Internet to cheer myself up and the good thing abt buying things off Ebay Joe is that you forget abt it as soon as you click pay so when the postman comes the next again week it is like a secret gift from an admirer instead of something you bought yourself because you were so depressed. But it is not reely a long term solution Joe and I am as much in the hole as ever now if not more so.

Of coarse the + side to going back to the club is that now I have a chance to get some appearance money etc under my belt or at lease you woud have thought so seeing as the club has 0 midfeilders left and the whole point of bringing me back is to put me in the team but if that is how your brane works Joe you woudent have won no manager of the month award in February as old Donaldson has put me back into the youth team on acct my fitness is not what it shoud be and he says I will be part of the squad for the next few weeks as they are down to the bear bones but I shoud not expect to actually play. Well what do you think abt that for manager motivation Joe to tell a player their is no chance of him getting a game and I feel like trying twice as hard now just to prove that he is wrong.

The youth team finish training earlier than the seniors Joe so I went over to watch them this afternoon and between you and me it is certainly not a case of absents makes the heart grow fonder. They have not improved 1 bit sints I left and if anything the standards have went right downhill. You will probily not have heard abt this Stephen Burdon character that they have signed Joe who is suposedly the next big thing but every manager in the league is trying to get ahead of the curve and if the next trend in Scottish football is for midfeilders with legs like fork prongs and hair like Tintin old Donaldson will be haled as a visionary and I will say 1 thing abt this Burdon guy Joe and it is that if he was choclate he woud eat himself and that is the 1 thing I have to say abt him.

Ater training was finished old Brady came on over and he shook my hand and said well well the wanderer returns which was a new 1 on me Joe and I guess he got me good with that. He asked me if I had got on ok at East Kilbride and why I was not training or had I enjured myself walking in the door like everybody else and I said no but old Donaldson has me working with the kids and Brady shook his head and said probily the kids get treated more like adults than the seniors do and that ever sints Burdon arrived everybody has to watch everything they say on acct that he is a proper snake who woud dob his own grandma in at the drop of a hat. So I said that he has not got no left foot neither and Brady said oh no he is a good player all right but there is more to a good team than just good players and take you for instants you coud maybe stand to loose a lb or 12 and you might have a big mouth but at lease you only use it for getting rid of donuts that is going spare and not for running your yap off abt who said what abt who.

Well Joe I guess when I am captain of the club I will go abt it a diffrent way and not just strut around running people in to the ground all the time and as for Burdon being a good player well I have seen better players playing penny whistle outside Foot Locker but it does not seem right to hall me back from EK when I was doing well just to have me play 2nd fiddle and I bet old Mackinnon woud flip his lid to see me being treated like this when he coud have used me for the title run in. But this is the problem with being a professhunal Joe and there are people out there who think that just because they pay your wages it means they own you same as how your manager at Tesco used to make you take your lunch in the cleaning cupboard so that you woud still be their if they needed you and I guess it is not as bad as that but it is still against my human rights as far as I know and I am not going to sit their quitely and take it. I am not reely sure what to do abt it just now tho because I cant afford a lawyer and I did think abt calling the cops Joe and I got as far as putting the first two 9s into my phone but I am not sure what they coud do abt it either so I am just going to lay low for the next few days and lull them in to a false sents of security and I do not know what I will do after that Joe but whatever it is it will be the last thing they woud of expected.

Your pal,

Andy


March 18th

Well Joe old Donaldson named the squad for this Satterdays game and I am in it. I guess that is a little bit of vindicashun for all my hard work sints I got back and it just goes to show Joe that you shoud never give up on your dreams altho of coarse Joe it is not true for everybody and for some people it woud probily be best to reign in your expectations a bit and not hope for too much and that way you wont be so dissappointed.

The game is away to Ross Country and is a twelve noon kick off so we will be travelling up on Friday night and sleeping in a hotel. The other lads dont like staying away from home and they were all mumping and moneing on acct that they will miss there familys etc but we are not away for long and at lease when they are home they have got their wifes to look after them but I do not Joe and hotels are the only chance I got to have someone else take care of me for a change.

So I am looking forward to it Joe even if they are not and the only down side is that the club are too mean to spring for a room each so we are haveing to share and my roommate is a lad the club just signed from France and his name is Vidian. Apparently he plays for Guadeloupe Joe which goes to show you what the standard of football is over their as he does not know what direction we are shooting ½ the time altho that is maybe on acct he does not speak any English. But it takes all sorts as they say Joe and he has not done me no harm and in fact he never says anything to anybody so I will probily be able to get threw the whole weekend without even noticing he is their and I guess he will be glad to have me as a roommate too instead of 1 of these other loud mouths that has always got so much to say for themselfs.

Burdon has got a room to himself of coarse and Brady says it is because no one else will room with him but to me Joe it is just pure favritism and it is old Donaldsons way of letting me know that I am still person non grata round this club and that he is only keeping me in the squad on acct that the owners woud scream blue murder if he left me out.

I do not know if I coud ever get a job as a scout Joe on acct that I do not have a face like a burst melodian but if I did I woud be prity good at it on acct I can look at any player in the world and tell you why they are no good. Now that I am back training with the 1st team I have been able to have a good look at this Burdon guy and for all the talk of him being a wonder kid and a golden boy etc Joe I can read him like a book and the only reason he is able to get by in this league is because people buy in to the hype and they have not got the sents to see threw it all like I have eg whenever he is on the right hand side he goes to cross with his right foot then faints and cuts inside. Well Joe our players is so dumb that he coud have a thought bubble comeing out of his head with a picture of him cutting inside in it and they still woud be none the wiser but once he comes up against 1 of these big guys at the proper teams they will go right threw him the 1st time he tries it and they might not even wait until then if they happen to here him speaking first as he is a proper no user Joe and you can take that from me.

For example Joe at training this am I had a chance to put 1 in to the near post and so I took it and as usual no one was on the same page and it went strait in to the keeper and Burdon threw his hands up in the air and said I am right here why dident you cut it back and I told him I dident see him and he said you woud have seen me if I had been between 2 slices of bread and then he says I know you are desprit for money but we dont get goal bonuses for training and I told him it was a pass not a shot and he said I coudent tell the diffrents which I guess goes to show you how much he knows abt football Joe.

Well I have got a prity good read on old Donaldson by now Joe and I already know that I wont be starting the game agenst Ross Country but he will put me on with 15 minutes to go just so he can say afterwards well I gave you a chance in the 1$^{st}$ team and you dident take it. Well Joe whenever you see 1 of these supersubs or impact players or whatever they are called all it reely means is they have got no football brane at all and it doesent matter to them what point of the game it is as they are just going to do the exact same thing irregardless. But a player like me that actually thinks abt the game needs time to feel things out and probe at the other teams weakness etc and it is no good throwing us in with 15 minutes to go and if you were fighting against an alien invasion Joe and you had Steven

Hawkings in your team it is obvious you woud have him involved from the start makeing plans and working things out etc and you woud not just wait until the aliens had almost landed and then shove a rifle in his hands and push him out the door.

Well Joe I will try and let you know how we get on but by all accts Ross Country is a prity small place and you can only get on the Internet their when your phone is plugged in to the wall so you might not here from me until Sunday but the game is on tv Joe so I am sure you will be tuneing in anyway to see your old pal Andy back in action and make sure the Selkirk chareman puts the game on in the clubroom Joe as if it was up to him their woud be nothing on any tv channel in the world exept horse racing and Diagnosis Murder.

Your pal,

Andy



March 20th

Well Joe I guess you already seen what came off this afternoon and how Ross County ever managed to lose to us I will never know. We had 2 shots on target and scored them both and Ross County had abt 20 and never even came close and of coarse I might as well have been watching the game with you back in Selkirk for all the diffrents it woud of made sints the closest I got to getting on was when I cut across the corners wile I was warming up and if there is 1 thing I have never understood abt football Joe it is why managers make you go and warm up when they already know you are not getting on especially when you are at an away game and all you get on your way around is showers of abuse. Of coarse I am a big boy Joe and to me it is just water off a ducks back but I hate to think that the supporters think it bothers me.

I guess the good thing abt being on the bench Joe is that you are able to get ready quicker and that way you are able to get on the bus 1st and choose the best seats. The other players all stampede strait up the back like it is a school trip to the zoo but for some reason Joe I have always prefered to sit up near the front. You cant sit right in the front 2 rows because that is where old Donaldson and his cronies mooch around but I got on early and got myself a nice seat in the 3$^{rd}$ row next to the isle so that it is too much bother for anyone to sit next to me and then everybody else got on all at once and there was the usual argy bargy abt who was sitting where and wile all that was going on Vidian turned round in the isle and hit me on the back of the head with his bag and sat down a couple of seats away.

Well Joe it was a sore 1 alright and I dont know why he needs all those horseshoes in his bag just to play football but that sort of thing happens all the time on the bus and usually you think nothing of it and I was just abt to sit back and open a packet of crisps when old Brady leaned across the isle and said that was a right haymaker big Vidian wapped you there Andy what have you done to upset him. Well Vidian was my roommate last night as you know Joe but I dident do nothing that coud of upset him and he hardly said 2 words the hole night he just lay their on the bed reading a book in French and laughing like this *heh heh heh* but he dident say a word so I just lay in my bed and watched tv until it was time to sleep. So I told Brady all that and he said well there is your problem right there in Vidians culture you are not allowed to have anything electrical turned on after 8pm and probily he thought you were disrespecting him by having the tv and the lites still on so I guess it is no wonder that he is so furious at you.

Well Joe that is the first I had heard of any of this and I told that to Brady and he said well I guess that is true but when Vidian 1$^{st}$ joined we had a team meeting to explane to us all abt his culture and how in Guadeloupe their are all kinds of things which mean 0 to you and me and we woud not even think twice abt them but they are a mortal offence to Vidian and to him it woud be as if I had spat on his grandfathers grave. So I asked Brady why Vidian dident say anything at the time and Brady laughed and said he expected that it was on acct that Vidian does not speak English altho it probily woud not have mattered any way and once you have done something like this to Vidian you have crossed a line that no amount of talking is going to fix and that the only reason we were able to afford him at all was because a couple of players from his old club had gone missing and his club wanted him off there hands before any more lives were lost.

Well Joe I dident say anything for a wile after that and then Brady patted me on the shoulder and said well I woudent worry too much abt it as the rules abt murder over here are a lot tougher than the ones in France and over their life does not have much value and a couple of people going missing is neither here nor there but over here the police take it quite seriesly if someone gets murdered and hopefully someone will have explained that to Vidian when he arrived and told him that he woud have to reign it in a bit. Then Brady said I guess if he was going to kill you he woud of done it last night when you lease suspected so I supose that means you are in the clear altho of coarse he will probily be keeping a close eye on you to make sure that you are toeing the line from now on so if I was you I woud just be careful and stick to the rules that we was told.

Then Brady picked up his newspaper and was abt to read it and I said to him but I wasent here when we were told the rules and Brady looked quite serious and said well there was an awful lot of them and in fact we spent a whole day in a classroom just to get the jist so I guess the best thing you can do is to watch what Vidian does and do exactly that same thing and as long as you do you cant go too far wrong.

Well Joe when Vidian got off the bus again he did not even look at me so I guess it is true what Brady says. Of coarse I am sorry if I have offended him and I certainly did not mean to and I will try not to do it again but it woud be nice if he was as offended when someone brushes him off the ball as he is by his own teammates who mean him no harm.

Your pal,

Andy

March 23rd

Well Joe people in the news are always talking abt how stressful it is to work in a hospital etc and how drs and nurses shoud get payed the same as footballers instead of a 1000 times less and I am not saying that is right Joe and I am not saying it is wrong but what I am saying is that at lease drs and nurses get a brake from the life or death decisions every now and then but for this last week I have felt like my life is hanging in the balance every second of the day and I am going crazy with it Joe and I am starting to feel like shooting myself in the head and getting it over with before anyone else gets the chance.

I told you already Joe abt how this Vidian guy has got the wrong idea abt something I did when we were in Ross Country and Brady told me the best thing I can do to temper his rage is to copy everything he does and that way I wont go wrong. Well Joe that is exactly what I have been doing at training this past week and I have left no stone unturned as they say. I know that diffrent people have got diffrent rules abt what you shoud and shoudent eat and so I have been having the exact same lunch as Vidian every single day and even eating it in the same order as him and all I can say Joe is that mashed potato with ketchup must be some kind of luxury item in Guadeloupe the way old Vidian wolfs it down and if I never see another sliced carrot in my life it will be too soon. I guess that is how come he is such a big guy Joe and he is abt the fittest player I have ever seen in my life only it is a shame there is no end product at the end of it otherwise the rest of us woud not have to bother showing up on a Satterday.

So I have been sticking to everything Vidian does Joe even the way he puts his kit on and it was working reely well to begin with Joe and he never paid me no mind and a couple of times when I was lining up behind him in the dinner hall he even smiled and gave me the nod but now I feel like it has stopped working and I have maybe missed something important because to begin with when I was going to the bathroom at the same time as him he never paid no notice but now he is starting to give me these reely funny looks and I am not sure if it is on acct I have done something else to offend him Joe or if there is something abt my bathroom routine that he does not like and today when I walked in to the toilet he watched me like a hawk the whole time Joe and it felt like I was sitting an exam only

at the end of it instead of Mr Browning saying well
Andy maybe we just have to accept that English isent
the subject for you I was going to get ripped lim from
lim and throne in to a pond. So of coarse I was so
nervous I walked out without washing my hands or
doing my fly up and I am sure that is another big strike
against me as far as Vidian is concerned and I am at my
wits end with the whole thing now Joe and I have tried
talking to Brady abt it again but all he says is that
everybody can tell how alarmed Vidian is getting at my
behaviour and the whole squad is on edge waiting to
see what is going to happen and that it woud maybe be
best all round if the whole thing just came to a head
now and run its coarse altho of coarse he understands
why I woud want to hang on in their and put off the
inevitable for as long as possible.

Well Joe I was so desprit that I was even thinking
abt learning French just so that I coud explane to
Vidian that he had got the wrong idea abt me and I was
always prity good at languages in school no matter what
old Browning said and I even started prepairing last
night by watching Amelie with the subtitles switched

off and I think I kind of got the jist of it Joe altho I dident totally understand why she was so into the photo guy as he seemed a bit simple to me but I supose you will never reely get 100% of what is being said in a film Joe even if it is in plain old English.

But anyway Joe it looks like it is has all been for 0 as we are away up to Inverness this Satterday and I have been put in a room with Vidian again and when old Donaldson read out the rooms I was looking strait at Vidian to see his reaction and when he turned round and looked at me looking at him his face was a picture Joe and you know how they say a picture is worth a 1000 words Joe well it dont take no 1000 words to tell what that picture means me for me Joe and just 3 will do it in this instants and they are good nite Andy.

Well Joe I dont know if theys Internet is any better up in Inverness but I will try to keep in touch if I can and let you know what is happening and if you coud turn on the tv in the clubroom at 3pm and check that I am in the line up for the game you will at lease know wether I made it threw the night and I am relying on you Joe because if the police in Inverness are anything like theys football team Vidian coud be wareing my corps as a poncho and they woud hold a press conference to say they had no leads.

Your pal,

Andy


March 25th


Well Joe as is now par for the coarse we got a lucky draw against Inverness even tho I did not get on and Inverness will not be able to believe that they did not win this game and the amount of bad luck they had they will need to win 3 lotterys in a row to make up for it. Having said all that when we saw them in the car park in the am I thought it was 1 of there cup winning teams from the Sixties who were meeting up for an anniversary luncheon but they still woud of beat us if old Brady had not lucked in a free kick in enjury time and by then the old fellas were dead on there feet Joe and I expect they went strait back to the retirement home rec room afterwards to sit down with a cup of tea and watch a John Wayne video.

Well the only thing you can say abt it Joe is that it was a stirring fight back and when we went 2 down with 20 minutes left Burdon suddenly started winceing and he did the exact same face you did that time you got stung on the inside of the knee by a wasp and signed to the bench that he woud have to come off tho of coarse Joe their was no danger of my being the 1 who came on. Well Burdon came and sat down on the bench and started talking reely loudly abt how he had done his hamstring covering for Brady and maybe he woud get a bit of football played if he wasent having to do all that running etc and in the middle of it all I gave a big yawn and Burdon turned round in his seat and said what are you yawning abt I guess you are exausted from all those walks to the pie shop.

Well Joe of coarse it was not that at all but I had been shareing a room with Vidian the night before and I had come up with a prity good plan to stop him getting to me which was to put an OUT OF ORDER sign on the bathroom door and barracade myself in their for the night and so I had rushed up to the hotel room as soon as we arrived and locked myself in to the bathroom but the only thing is Joe that I forgot to take in any blankets or pillows or food or anything and I spent most of the night trying to drink water out of the tap without making much noise and listening at the door for Vidian to leave but he dident make a peep the whole time and meanwile I was lying their in the tub beneath a towel and not hardly able to get a wink of sleep.

Well Joe I was not going to tell Burdon any of that so I just said that I had not slept well last night and he laughed and said oh yes I guess you were sitting up all night watching for Vidian in case he murdered you in your sleep and the only thing abt this club more embarassing than Brady and his pranks is you keeping on falling for them and there is only 1 person at this club who has not been laughing at you behind your back this whole week and no prizes for guessing who and Vidian is so scared of you following him around stareing at him that he paid for his own hotel room last night rather than room with you which I guess is what you woud have done if you had not been such a cheap skate and then old Donaldson turned round and he said thats enough now Burdon and Burdon dident say anything else after that but just sat their looking at me with that stupid little smile on his face.

Well his face dropped prity quick Joe when we came back from 2-0 down without him and you coud see he was stewing in it all the way back to the changeing rooms. So I got my stuff together ready to go but then Burdon made as if he was surprised to see me and he said where are you going shoudent you be in the shower scrubbing Vidians back and Brady looked up from his laces and said you know what Burdon its a shame your heart is not as $\frac{1}{2}$ as big as your mouth otherwise you woud be playing for Barcalona by now. Well Burdon just laughed and he said I guess heart is what you call it when someone jogs around for 90 minutes with their cheeks puffed out like big red balloons eh Brady.

Well Joe everything went quiet after that until Brady shook his head and went back to his boots and said well Burdon all I can say is I hope you get your big move sooner rather than later because a club like ours is no place for a big shot like you and Burdon smiled and said you can say that again chum and then old Donaldson came in and gave us a speech abt the game as if he was telling us abt a movie he had just seen that nobody else had and you coud not tell whether he was praising us to the skys or tearing a strip off us and I guess he did not reely know himself which it was. But whichever it was Joe it was not my idea of fun and I never thought I woud see the day but I woud give my front teeth to be back at East Kilbride again and anyway I woud fit in better there without them.

Your pal,

Andy


March 27th


Well Joe old Donaldson just phoned and he said the club is suposed to be sending 1 of our players along to open a new hairdressers that is starting up on Byres

Road so rather than come in to training tomorrow he woud like me to go and do the honours as they say.

Well of coarse Joe the way things are right now I woud much rather not go to training ever again and old Donaldson was nice as pie abt it so plenty of other players woud have taken it at face value and thought he was doing them a good turn but I know the old guy back to front by now and the only reason he is sending me is that I am the only player in the 1$^{st}$ team squad that has got any hair left and if he had asked Brady or Drummond or whoever to go and open a hairdressers they woud have said what the hell is a hairdressers.

Their is no extra money in it for me Joe altho I guess I might get a free haircut or 2 out of it at that and it will be kind of funny for me to be a celebrity Joe but it will probily be hard for you to imagine when the only time you have opened up a shop is when you are working the morning shift at the rotisserie. I will maybe even be able to give them some busness advice for example I have noticed there are lots of students around Byres Road so they shoud come up with some special deals on haircuts for students. These are the kinds of details that can make the diffrents between a successful busness and a 1ˢᵗ year failure.

Well Joe I supose I shoud wash my hair tonight so I wont have to do it tomorrow and if there is a story abt it on the tv or in the newspapers or anything I will send you a link so you can show off to your friends altho I guess most of them were my friends 1ˢᵗ and reely only talk to you because of me. But I supose if you share it on facebook you will get as many likes as if you had actually achieved something for yourself and that is the best way of looking at it from your point of view Joe.

Your pal,

Andy

March 29th

Well Joe when you hear all these celebritys moneing abt being famous it is usually hard to feel sorry for them but after todays shinanigans I dont blame them 1 bit and if you coud be famous in your own house without haveing to go outside or do anything I woud take that any day of the week after everything that has happent today.

Because 1$^{st}$ of all Joe the shops on Byres Road are weird and they go like this hairdresser record shop hairdresser fast food hairdresser hairdresser hairdresser record shop. It is what we in the busness call a saturated market Joe and if their are already a lot of 1 particular shop eg a hairdressers but none of another kind of shop eg charity shop then it stands to reason you shoud open a charity shop rather than a hairdressers so that you will get all the customers to yourself. But it seems like nobody in Byres Road has ever thought of that and I do not know how there are any shops left open the way they carry on.

Well Joe I was running a bit late on acct my 1$^{st}$ bowl of cereal dident reely fill me up and I had not expected their to be so many hairdressers so I was kind of running down Byres Road looking in the window of every barbers shop to see if it was the right 1 and I stuck my head in the door of 1 that kind of looked a bit shambolic and said did this hairdressers just open today and the hairdresser looked as if he wanted to kill me but I payed him no attention Joe on acct the guy whose hair he was cutting was him that does the football on the tv only I dont remember his name.

Well Joe he noticed me looking at him so he turned round and looked at my tracksuit and he laughed and said well well a couple of wins on the board and suddenly all the team colours come out eh and I laughed as if I thought what he said was funny and he said you been supporting them long and I said well actually I play for them and he said oh right the under 18s and I said no I am Andy Fairbairn and he kind of looked at me funny after that and turned back round and I guess it shows you what kind of an expert these guys are Joe when they dont even know the players names and a year from now he will be talking abt me as if he has been following my career right from the start Joe but you and I will both know what a phony he is.

Well Joe after that I was a bit out of breath on acct of all the running so I walked along the street looking for hairdressers and finely I found 1 with a pink ribbon across the door and a little crowd of people outside and there was a man with a big pair of scissors giveing a speech and I guessed he must be the owner Joe so I tried to give him a little wave to let him know I was here and he kept looking at me but not saying anything exept what he was already saying abt how exiting it was to be living his life long dream of opening a hairdressers and everyone laughed as if it was funny and so I did too only a bit louder than everyone else and it seemed like the owner had quite a bit more to say but then he changed his mind abt saying it and he just declared the hairdressers open and cut the ribbon and everyone cheered and went inside and so did I.

It seemed like everybody there knew everybody else but I dident know any of them so I was just walking around looking at things wile everyone was talking and drinking wine out of little plastic cups and I was pouring myself a drink and looking round to see if anyone had a notebook so that I coud tell they were from the newspaper when the owner walked up to me looking reely cross and he said well I am sorry you coudent hang on a couple of minutes wile I enjoyed the biggest moment of my life but it seems to me that if you have already waited 3 years to get your haircut you coud probily have held out for another 10 minutes and I said oh no I am not here for a haircut but I am here to open your hairdressers like the club sent me to do and he stared at me and he said well we waited ½ an hour for you to show up and you dident altho I guess you coud have been standing there the whole time and I woud have been none the wiser and just thought you were 1 of these fake big issue sellers you sometimes hear abt. Well thanks for nothing he said and I will be on the phone to your manager 1st thing to let him know what a grate job you have done of ruining my big day.

Well Joe I am not abt to take that from anyone and I woud have stormed out only it was such a pokey wee place that there was not even room to walk around in. So I had to sort of sidle out between all the people and when I got out I realised that I still had the open wine bottle in my hand but I was not going to take it back after all that Joe so I just kept walking and just as I was going past the other hairdressers the football guy from the tv walked out and I tried to hide the bottle behind my back Joe but I am sure he saw it and I tried to catch up with him and explane but I was out of breath from all the running around Joe and he was walking too fast so he got away.

So the whole thing was a complete wash out from start to finish Joe and I guess the moral of the story is that you shoud never do anyone a good turn for nothing as they will always just throw it back in your face and so will the media.

Your pal,

Andy


March 31st


Well Joe finely I made my 1$^{st}$ appearance sints comeing back and I subbed on for Burdon for the last 10 against Motherwell. He coud not say a thing Joe as he had contributed exactly 0 and altho 10 minutes is not much time to make an impression it gets me a little extra cash and puts me 1 appearance closer to getting that contract extension. I have worked it out that I need another 9 games to get that extension Joe so I am a little bit away but if we keep our cup run going and I sneak in off the bench now and then it shoud be ok.

The only trouble is Joe we have got a free weekend this week on acct of the internationals and instead of letting me do things at my own pace like anybody else old Donaldson wants me playing for the u20s on Sunday to keep my match fitness up and of coarse they are playing a friendly away to EK as part of the opening of their new coffee machine or something. I guess old Donaldson thinks because I kind of liked the folk at East Kilbride that I woud want to go back there but that is like saying you enjoyed a piece of gum so you want to go on chewing it forever. I do not know if old Donaldson has got a pure brass neck and is not bothered by anything but he does not seem to understand that it is embarassing for people to move on to better things and then go back to where they came from and it was ok for EK to treat me like 1 of their own when I was there but now I am trying to get in to the mindset of a professhunal footballer and it is hard to do that when people keep comeing up to you and slapping you on the back and calling you obesotron 3000. It is not what I need at this stage of my development Joe plus I have got to give a presentation on busness at the collage next week and I have got to get my ducks in a line for that.

So I have made up my mind to say that I am enjured Joe but the only problem is it needs to be a short term enjury as we have got a cup game agenst East Fife on Wensday and old Donaldson says he is going to give a run out to some of the fringe players so I guess I have a good chance of starting that game and showing East Fife what they missed out on. Well I looked up short term enjuries on Google Joe and the 1$^{st}$ result was abt suspected concussion which is perfect as that way you are not reely lying as you are not even saying there is definitely something wrong with you only that their might be. So that will put me out of the match on Sunday but able to come back for the match on Wensday without old Brady or someone saying something sarcastic abt the wonders of modern medicine. It is a perfect solution reely Joe and I guess it is funny that I am using my noggin to get out of this game in more ways than one.

Well Joe I will leave off there as I have got that presentation for next week and I need to get cracking. It is on sound busness practice and looking around the class I am probily the only person there who has worked a day in their life so I shoud have plenty to tell them abt how a good busness works altho of coarse as I always say Joe every man is his own busness nowadays even teachers.

Your pal,

Andy

April 2nd

Well Joe when a manager makes a big song in dance abt who is playing in a game you woud think they woud be planning on putting in an appearance themselfs but I guess that woud show how little you know abt professhunal football as old Donaldson was nowhere to be seen and instead he sent his wee crony Jimmy to take the side at EK and not only that but the only person from the 1$^{st}$ team squad to be involved was me so I guess according to Donaldson even our substitute goalkeeper is more match fit than I am.

So I rung up old Jimmy this am to let him know I woudent be able to make it and he said oh aye what is the matter with you then and I told him abt the suspected concussion and he said yes you are not the 1$^{st}$ person to have suspected that but what are you suposed to have done to have caused it and I had not reely thought of that Joe and of coarse what woud have been best woud of been if I had pretended to get hit in the head at training last week but I dident and so the 1$^{st}$ thing I coud think of to say was that I had run in to a door frame and old Jimmy laughed and said yes I guess your head is big enough at that and I woud probily have bought your story hook line and sinker if it hadent been for the part abt you running. So listen Andy he said you reely shoudent be on your own if you have a suspected concussion and I guess you woud have seen that yourself when you looked it up on the Internet so get down here to the team bus and there are plenty of young lads here who woud be glad to keep you company and if you take a wee turn for the worst Hairmyres Hospital is only a hop up the road so we can get you rushed strait in and make it official.

Well I coud read between the lines Joe and it has come to a prity sorry state of affairs when your own asst manager does not believe you when you only say you might be enjured and I guess if I ever need to get out of a game I will have to bring my death certifikit in and even then they will say well lets give him the 1st half and see how it goes.

I guess it was ok to go back to East Kilbride at that Joe and they were pleased to see me even tho we beat them. I scored a prity good goal Joe and it woud be 1 for the highlights reel if they had cameras but out of respect for my old club I did not celebrate it which I thought was prity classy of me Joe but afterwards Duffy and the rest of them kept comeing up to me and asking why I did not celebrate and when I told them they laughed and said it is not the champions league Andy just a friendly to open a new kitchen and you will not score many more of those in your life so you shoud have just went nuts. Well of coarse Joe if I had celebrated they woud have said it is not the champions league final Andy just a friendly so you cannot win either way sometimes.

Well we stayed back in the clubroom for a wile and they had a ceremony for opening the new kitchen and Duffy told me that they had decided to name the new kitchen after me on acct of my massive contribution to it and I told ½ the people in the clubroom that including the local MSP before I realised Duffy had only been making a joke abt my eating too much and after that I tried to drop the hint to people that I had only been jokeing before but they did not seem to get it and if that is all it takes to be an MSP in this country Joe I coud be president inside a year.

They always say you shoud never go back Joe and I guess if you have burned your bridges it is a diffrent thing but whenever I have went back to 1 of my old clubs I have always enjoyed it exept if you count coming back to this club after my lone finished and I am starting to wonder if I shoud even bother trying to get an extension on my contract or just let it run out and move on in the summer for the big money. I told Brady that the other day and he pooled a face and said well if Real Madrid are going to sign you in the summer you shoud at lease make sure you are under contract with us so that we get some money for you and I supose he has a point their Joe but ultimately it is all abt looking after no 1 in this game and that it what I intend to do Joe even tho my squad no is 28 which makes no sents to anyone.

Your pal,

Andy


April 5th


Well Joe the cup run continues and I started against East Fife just like I thought I woud. We won 4-0 and old Donaldson did not say nothing afterwards but if he left me on for the full match he must of thought I was doing something right as I guess he woud have let something slip if I was not liveing up to his high standards.

You woud think a cup game woud be a high pressure situation Joe and I guess for most people it is but for me it was a walk in the park as they say and it was nice way to unwind after my presentation at the collage. There was a couple of people presenting before me Joe but they were not up to much and I did not hardly pay any attention to them as I was going over my notes and I was working so hard I did not even notice when the teacher said that the next presentation will be by Andy Fairbairn. Well Joe I have played football in front of 1000s of people and it is not nothing compared to getting up and talking for 5 minutes in front of just a couple dozen but I had written out what I was going to say beforehand and I gave it prity much word for word so here it is.

Ladies and gentlemen and Mrs McNab I woud like to thank you all for inviting me here today to speak abt the subject of busness. Now the Oxford English

Dictionary defines busness as a commercial operation or company but as we all know there is a lot more to it than that and I hope to be able to explane to you over the next 5 minutes why the world of busness can learn a lot from football.

Now as we all know profeshunal football is a busness and as a professhunal footballer it is my busness to put in the best possible performance for my employers because if you are not giving customers full satisfaction in your work then 99 times out of 100 you will wind up going bankrupt. As we are often told the customer is always right and that is true exept sometimes the customer gets it badly wrong and you just have to ignore him eg when your manager tells you only to do outswinging corners but the opposition goalie is just a little guy and reely you shoud be swinging them right in on top of him and knocking him abt a bit. So altho the customer is always right sometimes you have to ignore him and do your own thing and then tell him afterwards that you did what he said even if he says he watched you with his own eyes.

But what I am saying is that football is like a busness

and the clubs and leagues and the players are all their own busnesses and 1 of the key things abt being a busness is looking after your brand and not letting other people make you look like an idiot. Because when the big companys are looking out for people to advertise their cloths for example they want people who have put a bit of thought into how they dress and how they come over to the public and not people who are walking around for 20 minutes with a peace of toilet roll dangling from their trouser leg like a friend of mine back in Selkirk used to do. So you have got to be on the lookout for things that might damage your brand or make you look stupid as over the coarse of your career they coud wind up costing you millions.

The other thing I woud say abt football and busness is that in both football and in busness the numbers do not lie and if you want to get anywhere in either of them then you will have to pay attention to statistics. Altho sometimes the numbers will not look grate for someone on acct they are not getting enough game time and are not able to get into a settled rithim usually over the coarse of a career things will tend to average out and the cream will always rise to the top. But if the numbers tell you that such and such a player shoud be starting every week your busness will suffer if you ignore them for example if the goalkeeper in a penalty shoot out has dived to the right 3 times in a row it is obvious you shoud put the ball to his right as what are the odds that he is going to dive that way again. It does not make no sents for him to do that and it is not your fault if he does as it just means he is an actual psychopath and if everyone else had scored their penaltys it woud not even matter anyway.

So as you can see there are a lot of similaritys between football and busness but the main 1 in my opinion is that neither of them can be learned and you have either got a talent for them or you dont and if you dont there is no point makeing yourself miserable abt it but you shoud just do what my friend did and accept your limitations and find something else that you are better at altho to be fair busness and sport kind of cover a lot of ground and if you are not good at either of them you are probily not going to be much good at anything else either.

Well thank you for listening to me today and I will be happy to take any questions.

Well Joe as you can see I had prity much covered all the bases and I guess everybody was too busy thinking abt all the stuff I had gone over to ask any questions as there was some real brane teasers in their. But that is me Joe I shoot strait from the hip as they say and I do not get too bogged down in all the stuff abt employment law etc as to me that is just what people do to cover up for the fact that they do not reely understand the subject the same way that folk who do not know anything abt football are always talking abt putting the ball in the channel as if it even means anything.

Well Joe after my performance yesterday I will be amazed if I do not get a run out on Satterday altho I am amazed all the time here so I guess it wont make no diffrents but I will let you know how I get on and hopefully things are now back on track for the rest of the season.

Your pal,

Andy


April 8th


Well Joe I did make a little cameo against United and I came on for the last 15 minutes so the momentum is slowly building up and I guess at this rate when I am in my seventies my grandkids will be pulling me up out of my armchare and saying hurry up grandpa they are putting you on for the start of the 2$^{nd}$ half.

I guess I shoud not be running round the houses just yet Joe as it is only 15 minutes but just for a change I was not getting subbed on for Burdon as he was not playing and in fact he was stuck on the bench next to me for the entire game and did not get off it. I guess the golden boy has lost his shine eh Joe but old Donaldson did not look at him the whole game and now that I come to think of it nobody else spoke to him at all not even the once and if I had not known any better Joe I woud have thought that he was a figmint of my imagination only I hope my imagination woud come up with something a lot better than Steven Burdon Joe I can tell you.

I shoud not worry abt it Joe as it has 0 to do with me but it is strange to see how quickly someone can go from hero to 0 as they say and even wee Tony the kit man is looking strait threw him which is prity bad as normally Tony will talk the hind legs off a donkey and there are players at the club who plan their hole routeen around not bumping in to him in the corridor and listening to him tell them the entire plot of the film he was watching on tv last night which is always Casino Royal. But even wee Tony did not have no time for Burdon yesterday so things must be prity bad and I asked old Brady what Steven Burdon was suposed to have done wrong and Brady just looked at me and said Steven who so I went and checked on the teamsheet and his name is Burdon right enough but I guess Brady forgot on acct of all those head enjurys.

Anyway Joe what it adds up to is more game time for yrs truely only instead of putting me strait into the team old Donaldson has shifted things around to put an extra forward in and I have always thought that I would make a good target man Joe and when I said that to Brady and he said yes you would make a great hold up man and you prove that every month when you get your pay slip and the only thing you are missing is the black mask and the bag with swag written on it. So you never know Joe if Brady puts in a good word for me I might get a wee run out up front but if not it looks like I am now 1$^{st}$ in line for a spot in midfeild if anyone gets enjured or suspended or something only there is no danger of that with Brady Joe as he woud have to tackle someone first.

But the timing coud not be better Joe as we have our cup game this week and if we win that 1 we are through to the semis and then we have got our derby match comeing up next weekend and a decent result there woud put us in to the top 5 in the league and of coarse the bubble will burst soon enough Joe and old Donaldson will find a way to make things collapse around our ears but I reely need to get in to the 1$^{st}$ team picture while we are doing well because once things start to go pare shaped people will be looking around for escape goats and of coarse they woud never blame old Donaldson as he is totally untouchable but if some poor sap likes yrs truely has just came into the 1$^{st}$ team round abt then you can be sure he will be the 1 to carry the can.

You see Joe these are the sorts of things you have to think abt as a professhunal footballer and it is not all fun and games and you have got to have a bit of sents abt you and sometimes it can be best not to play when it is going to make you look bad and I was reading on the Internet the other day Joe abt this player who was a fraud and he kept getting signed by big teams and then mysteriously getting enjured before playing a game for them and he managed to make a whole career for himself and earn a bunch of money without ever kicking a ball and it made me think abt you Joe exept for the big teams and all the money.

But what I am getting at Joe is that football is not just abt playing well but abt playing well in the right place at the right time and with these 2 big games comeing up I woud say that now is the perfect time to start showing what I can do. So here I go Joe.

Your pal,

Andy


April 10th


Well Joe Burdon was nowhere to be seen at training this am and when I asked people where he was they said he was enjured all of a sudden and when I asked what kind of enjury he had Brady said there is a lot you do not know abt football Andy and some of it you are better off not knowing. Well Joe there is a lot he does not know abt what I know but I guess the bottom line is that Burdon is out of the picture and I have got a clean run at the 1$^{st}$ team. They have gived out the squad for the cup game at the weekend and I am in it Joe and I woud bet a £1 to a 1p that I will get on towards the end and that is when you want to be on the field during a cup match as nobody remembers the first 15 minutes of a big game only the last 15. So you probily do not need to tune in until abt 4:30pm Joe altho it is not as if you will have anything else to do anyway so I guess you might as well.

Your pal,

Andy

April 12th

Well Joe people are always going on and on abt the magic of the cup but I am not sure who exactly they are because everybody I know hates the cups and when you look at the faces of the people who have just been told they are in the squad for the cup game you woud think they had just been given free entry to the world cholera championships. Nobody in your team wants to play and nobody in the other team wants to play either exept for there is always 1 guy who did not get the message and thinks it is a big oppertunity to make a name for himself and is flinging himself into tackles and clapping his hands and shouting come on lads lets get in to this lot and the rest of his team are completely humiliated and trying to make it look like they do not know him. Then of coarse all of the supporters have suddenly got other things to do exept for the hardcore ones that is there threw thick and thin complaning there hearts out and the 1$^{st}$ thing they complane abt Joe is the weakened side that we are putting out and then they just sort of improvise from there.

Of coarse old Donaldson will not admit any of that Joe and he is acting like it is a big game for the club and I guess he has a point in so far as it is a quarter final and we are almost into the big money rounds and only 2 games from the final itself. Everybody always bangs on abt how important is for a club our size to get a good cup run going and put some money into the coffers but the thing is Joe but you never see a club doing well 1 year and say oh that must be on acct of all the money from there great cup run last year. When Selkirk got threw the first couple of rounds 2 years ago everyone said we woud be rolling in it but then fast forward to next year and we are still having cold stovies for tea and it is obvious Joe that the whole thing is just a swindle to make people think that the cup matters when it doesent.

Having said all that Joe you shoud never look a gift horse in the mouth and the only times I have started for the club have been in cup games and I should at lease get on off the bench this Satterday agenst Kilmarnock and that will take me a step closer to that new contract. Seeing what has happent with Burdon this week has reminded me how quickly things can turn against you in this game and obviously that will never happen to me Joe but it is better to have 1 bird in the hand than 2 in the bush so to speak. At lease if I get that contract extension I am certain of a wage next year and if another club is keen the fact that I am under contract wont stop them from swooping in and on these wages Joe they coud buy out my contract with the money they found in their denim jacket they have not worn sints last summer.

Well Joe I guess I shoud get some sleep before the game tomorrow as I am getting in the habit of staying up late just on acct that when you get to the end of the day and nothing worthwile has happent you feel kind of cheated and you wind up staying up for a few more hours just on the off chance that something will happen that made it worth getting up out of bed that am. But I guess that is just wishful thinking Joe and once it hits 2:30 in the am and you are still watching qvc you can probily write the whole thing off as a net loss.

Your pal,

Andy



April 13th



Well Joe as always with these cup games it all comes down to who wants it least and Kilmarnock are only 2 points off the bottom right now so the last thing they wanted was a semi final to worry abt. I woud never accuse another professhunal of takeing a dive Joe but when a midfeild is letting theirselfs be dominated by old Brady and Drummond you have got to ask a question or 2 tho of coarse by the time I came on they were playing out their minds and woud have run threw a brick wall to win the ball which is a disgrace when you think abt it Joe and I woud never let the supporters down like that unless their was a reely good reason but I guess that is why Scottish football is in the hole that it is in right now so to speak.

So we won prity much at a canter and old Donaldson was trying to put a brave face on it in the changeing rooms by talking abt what a credit we are to the club and how it is every supporters dream to follow their club to Hampden and thanks to us our supporters woud be liveing that dream but if he was happy abt it Joe he shoud have tried telling his face as he looked like he had missed the last bus tho on the plus side I did find out who it is has kept the magic of the cup line going all these years sints when our chareman came in to congratulate us he was just abt turning summersalts so it shows you how much these people know abt football Joe and I guess that is the problem the whole world over Joe which is that the people in charge are never at the top because they are good at something but because some money fell into their lap and they did not know what else to do with it.

Well Joe we move on and the derby match is the big

1 now altho personally I have never seen the value in all that local rivalry stuff and the only reason I ever cared abt beating Gala Fairydean was because they were a bunch of inbred weirdos with haircuts from the Eighties and not because I had anything against them in peticular.

Your pal,

Andy

April 17th

Well Joe no suprises for guessing what has been the mane topic of conversation at training this week and if I never here the words bragging rites again in my intire life it will be too soon. Never mind that there is not a player at the club who grew up within a 1 hundred miles of the ground Joe and that whenever some old club legend is brought into the changeing room to say hello he might as well be someones grampa that has got lost on his way to the toilet for all anyone here woud know but of coarse it is reely touching to see how desprit everyone suddenly is to put 1 over on our local rivals and even old Vidian is getting in on the act even tho if he got on the wrong bus tomorrow and wound up playing for the other lot he woud not be any the wiser and I am not having a go at him Joe as he does not know any better but for me Joe it just a game like any other and I am not going to spend any more time thinking abt it than I do any other game which is strickly 0.

It is an away game tomorrow Joe so even tho it is only 5 minutes up the road we have got to be up at the crack of dawn as they want us to get their nice and early in case there is any trouble. I guess you will remember that time we went to Gala Fairydean early for the same reason Joe and their was nobody at the ground when we got there and we had to stand outside until someone showed up to let us in and half of Galashiels walked past without saying so much as a word and the worse thing that happent was that someone wrote CLEAN ME in the dirt on our team bus. Well I guess passions run high during these darby matches Joe and we woud not want a repeat of anything like that tomorrow.

Your pal,

Andy


April 18th


Well Joe I guess you will already have seen what happent this pm you and everybody else in the country but I know you will have been waiting to hear the story strait from the lions mouth as they say so here it is Joe only it has taken me a little longer to write as it is hard to remember what order everything happent in.

Old Donaldson has been going big on the whole a darby is just 3 points like any other bit and all threw the warm up and the pre match talk he kept banging on abt not getting sucked in to a darby mentality and how the team that can rise above all that is the team that will win and then Brady got up and I thought we woud get some blood and thunder but instead he just picked up where old Donaldson left it and told us that we shoudent need a darby atmosphere to get ourselfs up for a game and that if the team in the other changeing room wanted to play with there hearts that was up to them but that we were going to get out there and play with our heads like we always do and everybody in the changeing room was nodding away and agreeing and by the end of it all Joe I was so pumped up I was only sorry I hadent brought some knitting along.

I guess I know quite a bit when it comes to football Joe but I am not too proud to admit that there are some aspecks of the game you know more abt than me and 1 of them is what it is like to not be in the team. If I am honest Joe I find it hard to get much out of the warm ups when I know I am not starting and it just seems pointless to go through all those drills and stretchs etc when you know it is going to be another 2 hours before you get anywhere near a ball and maybe longer. So I try to save my good stuff for when I am actually playing Joe and during the warm up everybody was getting on my case and saying what the hell whenever I played them a pass and when you think what a song in dance Brady was making in the changing rooms abt being calm and collected it seems funny to me that he woud be flipping his lid over a couple of overhit passes during the warm up by somebody who is not even going to be playing. I guess that is what we in the busness world woud call micro management and the advice that I woud have given Brady is to not sweat the small stuff but he did not ask for my advice Joe and he did not look like he woud appresiated it if I had given him it anyway.

It is quite weird to be playing in front of 1000s of supporters Joe and everybody always asks me what that is like and why I am not nervous and it is a funny thing Joe but to me it feels like the more people are watching me the less nervous I am abt it. If you are playing in the premier league and there are 10000 fans there well that is a lot of people Joe but at the end of the day you do not know any of them from Adam and you woud have to be some kind of rain man to focus on 1 of them in peticular and listen to what he was saying and care abt what he thought and sints your brain is not made up that way you just blank the whole lot of them out and that is that. It is diffrent when you are playing in front of 15 people at Selkirk on a Wensday night and 1 of them is your friends dad and he is leaning right over the railing and screaming in your ear every time you take a corner and then telling you every time he sees you for the next week you have got a foot like a thruppenny bit and you woud never have got a game under old Bully back in the Sixties. So it is funny when you think abt it Joe but it is quite a bit harder to ignore 1 person saying you are rubbish than a 1000 people saying it.

Well to be honest with you Joe that is not reely a problem I have had so far at the club and in fact it has been hard to get people to have an opinion abt me 1 way or the other and when old Donaldson got me stripped to go on for the last 15 minutes wile it was 1 goal a peace I heard the grones from around the ground and I guessed it was because we were replacing an attacker with a midfielder rather than because they have got anything in peticular against me. But even at that Joe there was only a little grumbling and you woud think that if the manager was happy to take 1 point in a darby match when his team are on the front foot he woud get pelters for it but I have been reading up on all the forums abt what these fans think of Donaldson and they basicly think he can do no wrong and if anybody comes on to the boards playing devils advocat so to speak and trying to get a little bit of discussion going they just get shot down strait away which I guess goes to show you Joe that all this talk abt freedom of speech on the Internet is not what it is cracked up to be.

But I will give old Donaldson his dews Joe and before I went on he said that Brady and Drummond were running out of steam and he wanted me to push forward and put a bit of pressure on their back 4 to try and take the heat off and of coarse if he thought Brady and Drummond were struggling the sensible thing to do woud have been to take them off but then he woud be admitting that he had made a mistake and if I have learned 1 thing abt football these past few years it is that there is not a manager in the world who woud not rather slit his wrists with a rusty knife than admit that he was wrong abt something. So I am on a hideing to 0 Joe and all the advice old Donaldson has got is to make a nuisance of myself which is a bit like telling the

Rolling Stones to get up there and fill in the silences.

So on I go Joe and 1 of their center backs turns to the other and says bloody hell its Spongebob Squarepants and I just let them laugh it up Joe as I do my talking on the pitch exept with me I do it by scoring goals and sometimes by assisting them. So they might have thought it was funny when I came on Joe but the good thing abt being an unknown quantity is that nobody knows how to handle you or what to expect or even what position you play so they were expecting me to come on as a strait replacement up front and when I dropped off into the hole they dident know whether to follow me or let me be and it wasent long before I had them cursing and swearing and turning themselfs inside out trying to pick me up and of coarse that gave us the numbers on them in midfeild Joe tho I guess some of this is quite technical stuff and I do not reely expect you to understand it.

But even you will be able to understand what happened right at the end Joe and Donaldson told us before the game that their left back was the weakest link and all game our out ball was to put it in the space behind him and 9 times out of 10 he would bombscare it out and that is how we got our corner kick. Well being honest Joe I had kind of forgotten what I was ment to be doing at corners as I am so used to takeing them myself but I figgered their goalkeeper was not the best and neither was their defence or any of our attackers and so there was a prity good chance no one woud get anything on the cross when it came in and it woud go strait threw the whole lot of them and so I made a gamble Joe and pooled off to the far post and sure enough the ball went right threw and I did not even have to get up off the ground but instead I just side footed it in easy as you like.

Well Joe their was absolute bedlam and the fans went crazy and I thought that 1 of their players was attacking me but it was just old Brady giving me the big splash and before I knew it the whole lot of them was on top of me Joe and I am used to carrying a whole team Joe but it would take a Pickfords truck to lift this lot and when I got out from under them I was so dizzy and lightheaded that the game was finished before I remembered where I was.

It is kind of a spacy feeling to score a goal like that Joe and the only thing I can remember is Brady grabbing me at the end of the game and pulling me over to where our fans were and they started singing my name and I guess I still felt a bit faint Joe because I teared up a bit and then again when I got back to the changeing room and everybody stood up and applauded and even old Donaldson put his hand on my neck and said enjoy this feeling son because it is a once in a lifetime.

After the game all the reporters wanted to talk to me and to be honest with you Joe I was a bit overwhelmed and I kept saying the same things over and over and once I was finished Donaldson and Brady pulled me into the office and old Donaldson explained to me that their woud be a lot of people trying to get their claws in to me for the next week or so and that I shoud be careful who I speak to and what I say. Then Brady piped up and he said probily I felt on top of the world right now and I had earned it but that it woudent last and that after a wile people woud start to lose intrest and I shoudent get too caught up in it as nothing derails a young footballers career like a big goal that makes him think he has got it made.

Well Joe I acted as if I was listening and I guess there are some players who have been tripped up that way and have caught a lucky break and then not had nothing to back it up with but I am not in that boat Joe as I have plenty more in my locker and all I needed was the platform to show people that and now I have got it. In fact I have hardly been able to write this email for my phone ringing off the hook and already I have had 2 calls from newspapers wanting to interview me and 1 of them was old Macky at the Selkirk Advertiser so it shows you how quickly people change there tune. I guess 1 or 2 reporters might even get in touch with you as well Joe just to hear the 1$^{st}$ hand scoop abt how I came from nowhere as they say and if you do speak to anyone Joe I know you will do your old pal Andy proud only I hope you will not mention anything to do with the senior prom Joe as that is all ancient history now and it is no good to anybody to go dredging all that up again.

Your pal,

Andy

# Remember the Time

April 20th


Well Joe it has been some weekend and old Donaldson was 100% right abt the media hype and I bet that hairdresser in Byres Roads is beside himself thinking abt what he has missed out on and a picture of me opening his smelly old barbershop woud be worth its weight in gold now but I guess their has always got to be a villain of the peace Joe and these are the kinds of things that drive you on to grater and grater success like I am doing.

Of coarse at training it was strait back to busness as usual Joe and I might as well have come in with a clipboard and a Unicef tee shirt on for all the reaction I got and there have been a couple of wise cracks abt my being on tv but it has all been prity tame Joe which is a bit funny on acct that when you score the winning goal in a big darby match nobody has got a word to say but when you turn up to training eating a choc ice once everybody is talking abt it for weeks.

On the + side Joe it seems like old Donaldson is

starting to draw me in to the inner circle a bit and at every training session there are players who treated like players and players who are treated like training accesories and up until now I might as well have been a traffic cone with a face painted on for all the diffrents it made but the last couple of days he has been takeing me to 1 side and giving me a few pointers here and there Joe and it is nothing I hadent already heard when I was playing for Selkirk u14s but it is good to know that I am in his thoughts as they say and I guess he will be anxious to get me tied down to a new contract now that the wolfs are at the door. Everything he says now begins if you want to make a career in this game or you have a bright future ahead of you Andy so long as you remember and I guess he is looking forward to 5 years from now when the only job he will be able to get is on the radio and the only reason he will be able to get that is because he has got so many storys abt coaching Andy Fairbairn. Well it will all be beneath my notice by then Joe and it will be water off a ducks back as their will just be too many people trying to claim a peace of me for me to put them all in their place.

Anyway Joe old Donaldson keeps telling me that the important thing is not to get carried away and that their will be pressure on him to play me and a lot of managers woud throw me strait in at the deep end just to save there own skins but that he is going to do right by me and by the club by bringing me along a bit at a time. Well Joe we will just have to see what the supporters say abt that and their has been some buzz around me on the forums and a lot of people are wondring why they have not heard of me before which I guess is there way of asking why old Donaldson hasent been playing me and it looks like their will be a few supporters making their views known abt it if I am not in the team on Satterday. Well Joe they are paying customers and that is their right tho most of them know as much abt football as if they were aliens who had found out abt it by reading Oor Wullie but it does not take no brane surgin to look at me and old Brady and tell which 1 shoud be playing professhunal football and which 1 shoud be standing at the bar watching it on the tiny wee screen with the sound turned down.

Well Joe I started writeing this an hour ago and I

have already had 2 missed calls so I guess I shoud get back to the grindstone as they say. I will write to you again once things have quieted down a bit.

Your pal,

Andy


April 23rd


Well Joe you have got to hand it to old Donaldson right enough and when he sets his mind to something you can be sure he wont do it by halfs and a week after scoring the winning goal in the biggest match of the season guess who is left sitting on the bench until the last 15 minutes but yrs truely. I coud not believe it when he read out the teamsheet before the game and I thought maybe he had read out an old 1 or got my name mixed up with someone else so I went up and asked him just to be sure and he looked at me as if I was crazy and said that we had been over all this and that I woud not be starting any games until he was sure

I was good and ready.

Well when he sent me off to warm up I made sure and wetted the fans appetites by going right around the pitch and everywhere I went I got a nice round of applause and the same again when I went on so it shows that at lease a few 1000 people have not forgotten what I have done for this club. I played a prity good game once I got on and even Donaldson admitted that himself so hopefully the pressure is mounting as they say and I have got to stay in the picture if I am going to get this contract extension.

It is kind of a shame that the club has been so lucky this year Joe and we have not been relegated yet as if their was nothing left to play for then Donaldson woud not reely have any option exept to start looking to the future but as long as we are still in the running to stay up he will keep shoving out the same 11 week after week. I guess all I can do Joe is make the most of it whenever I am out there and show the supporters what they are missing so that they put the pressure on Donaldson to play me from the start tho of coarse that is difficult Joe as fans are so ignorant abt football nowadays and today I run past 2 defenders and played a perfect ball into space and the fans applauded it like I was a 5 year old that had just finished singing Jingle Bells for the 8$^{th}$ time in a row. I supose I woud understand it if they had been watching Barcalona for the last few years but old Brady has been here all his life so there is probily nobody alive who remembers when the clubs out ball wasent a scuff pass hit to the keeper. But that is football as they say Joe and sometimes you are wasting your breath trying to explane it to people especially when all they are bothered abt is wether or not you are picking up your man.

Things have gone quiet on the media for now but that is just on acct that it is the weekend and there is some actual football to report on. To be honest Joe I am kind of glad as it is not as much fun as I thought it woud be on acct that the reporters do not reely care what you have to say. I always thought you coud only get a job writing abt football if you liked it and were interested in it but when I am talking to reporters you woud think from their faces that I had walked into their living room and was standing in front of the tv wile eastenders was on. If they spent as much time listening as they do posing me for photographs then we woud finely be getting somewhere but I guess that is too much to ask Joe and I supose the readers woud not have a clue what I was banging on and on abt football for if their was not a picture of me leaning against a goalpost on the same page.

It is all valuble experience of coarse Joe but what I coud reely do with right now is valuble cash as there is not a month goes by without me losing money hand over fist and it seems like the insentives system here is left over from the old days when every game used to finish 15-8 and now that I have had my $1^{st}$ goal bonus I can tell you that I will need to average abt 6 goals a game in order to brake even. I only wish their was some way I coud get some money with no strings attached as I cannot afford to pay the intrest on another lone right now not if it is from a bank but if it was from a friend that woud be ok but I do not know hardly anybody who has that kind of money floating around Joe and I only wish I was living at home like you are and building up the savings instead of scraping around hoping that someone will offer me a few £100 just to keep me going say even £500 woud probily be enough altho obviously a £1000 pounds woud be better.

Your pal,

Andy

April 25th

Well Joe that has taken me a back as it did not never cross my mind but if you can spare the money I woud reely appresiate it. I woud never have asked but I guess you must have been able to tell that I was at my wits end and you can sure you will get it all back before long Joe because between you and me your old pal Andy is looking like a prity safe investment.

The reason I say that Joe is I got a phone call from an agent this am and I have decided to let him represent me. His name is Harry and he has dealt with footballers before but he also does other things like real estate and enjury compensation and for someone with like me who has a morgage and delicate ankles it woud make a lot of sents to have an agent who covers all the bases. The only thing is Joe he wants 10% of everything I make but that is after I hagled him down from 11% Joe so I have got a prity good deal and if he is able to find me a sponsorship deal or something it will be money well spent. I don't know if he is due 10% of the £500 you are giving me Joe but we will keep that between the 2 of us and what he doesent know wont hurt him as they say.

Well Joe I listened to what old Harry had to say and he told me that basicly whatever wages I am on right now they shoud be paying me twice that and if he was my agent he woud march right in there and demand a encrease in salary as he woud not let his clients have the micky taken out of them and that was all music to my ears Joe and there is no better way of describing what is happening right now than that I am having the micky taken out of me. So I have signed on with Harry to be my agent Joe and the only way from here is up but I will still need that £500 we talked abt so please send it as soon as possible and I will put it on the tab so to speak. Thanks Joe you are a pal alright.

Your pal,

Andy


April 27th


I dont know why I dident think of having an agent before Joe as it seems like kind of a no braner and old Harry has already got me a boot sponsor. I got a boot sponsor when I signed for the club as they have got a deal built in for all there u21s but to me Joe that does not reely count as sponsorship as the CEO at Adidas probily does not even know if I am alive or dead but when someone actually comes to you and asks you to wear there boots Joe that is a different story and it tells you something abt what they think of you as a player and how highly they rate you.

There is no money in it for now Joe just some free

boots and I guess that shows old Harry is out to do his best for me as he cannot exactly get 10% of my free boots and in fact he stands to make £0 out of this deal but I am a valued client of his and he has already said he woud sooner make no money out of me at all than see me sign a deal for less than I am worth so it shows you that for some folk it is not all abt the money Joe. I can think of quite a few people around this club that coud stand to lern something from Harry and of coarse money is important Joe but you shoud be able to set that to 1 side and concentrate on your football like I am doing and leave the money to the profeshunals altho of coarse Joe I have got a national certifikit in busness so I know as much as anyone abt making money and probily quite a bit more.

The new boots that Harry has got me are quite a bit better than the other ones Joe and it shows I am making waves when even Nike want to get a peace of the action but I wont need my old boots anymore Joe so if you woud like them I will send them to you as a gift altho if you wanted to knock £20 off the amount I owe you I woud not say no sints you woud be sitting on a proper gold mind if you hung on to them a bit. It woud be a waste for you to wear them Joe as it woud be kind of like giving a Ferrari to a sea lion but if you wait a year or 2 before selling them as match worn by Andy Fairbairn it woud wipe out the money I owe you 100 times over tho of coarse Joe I am not saying that you shoud count the boots agenst the £1500 I owe you just that it is something to think about is all.

I say that they are match worn Joe but thanks to old Donaldson that means they are basicly good as new. In the last 2 games I have only got 30 minutes and 20 minutes a peace altho I guess it keeps the appearance money flowing in and if I keep getting subbed on I shoud make my contract extension with a few games to spare. But even if I got enjured and did not make the 25 appearances it woud be a bit funny if the club did not renew my contract after their has been all this hype around me and a lot of people saying I am going to be the next big thing. I guess it woud look bad on the club if they let me go now and probily they will work something out with Harry no matter how things pan out with appearances.

Well Joe old Donaldson says that now I am a senior player and in line for a peace of the bonus money at the end of the season I will have to start pulling my weight a bit in terms of going out and representing the club. This is the time of the year when all the supporters clubs have their annual dinners etc and the club usually trys to send a player or 2 along but between me and you Joe I did not even know that we had a supporters club never mind more than 1 so I am not sure that is much of an issue. But the club sends players along to other events for charity and things like that and now I am graduated from collage I guess I dont mind going along to a coffee morning or 2 every now and again and shakeing a few hands as it is a big thrill for normal people to meet a professhunal footballer. Of coarse footballers are just normal people like anybody else Joe but supporters do not know that tho I guess they are not long in wiseing up once old Brady comes along with his wonky teeth and his head like a toilet brush.

So I was meant to have a day off tomorrow but it looks like I will be going to an event with a couple of the lads and Brady is picking me up 1st thing so you probily will not hear from me again until tomorrow pm but that is the life of a footballer Joe and if you cannot take the heat you shoud get out of the kitchen so to speak.

Your pal,

Andy


April 28th


Well Joe old Brady pulled up outside my flat 10 minutes early yesterday and I had not hardly got out of bed and when I went down he said you are not going out dressed like that when you are meant to be representing the club so I got changed and when I came back down Brady kind of pooled a face and said well I guess it is not Silk Purse FC we are playing for and at lease now you are wearing a club badge they will be able to tell you are not 1 of the patients. Well Joe with Brady making such a big fuss abt how I looked I had guessed we were going to the british embassy for a big reception but when he said that abt patients I put 2 and 2 together and realised where we were going and I asked him where we were going and he said the hospital and I said yes I thought so.

The only hospital I have ever been in Joe is the borders general hospital that time I broke my leg but they said I had only straned it and I can tell you Joe it is no suprise the people in the borders look like they do when you see the hospitals they have got up here and next to the hospitals in Glasgow the borders general looks like 1 of those burger vans you see in a layby on the road to Cornhill on Tweed. The hospitals here are big enough that they have separate places for separate enjuries so that everyone with heart problems is in one dept and everyone with broken bones is in another rather than it just being a free for all like the borders general where every ward looks like a scene from saving private ryan and when the 4 of us got there a woman took us up in a lift and told us what to expect and I supose she was a nurse Joe exept she dident have any nurse stuff on and she told us that a lot of people in the gerryatric ward were there because they were very old which is funny Joe as I thought maybe they were there on acct of having tennis elbow but anyway she said some them are perfectly sound but some of them get quite confused and it is best to deal with them with kid gloves so to speak and I said old Donaldson but then Brady stepped on my foot before I got finished.

Well Joe we went around the gerryatric ward saying hello to everyone that wasent asleep and most of the ones that wasent were quite happy to talk to us only I do not think they always knew who we were as they manely talked abt themselfs which kind of defeats the purpose in my eyes Joe as anyone can sit and listen to them talking abt themselfs and there is no need to drag professhunal footballers all the way there just for that. I found it quite hard to make conversashun with most of the old people Joe as I did not do history at school and I do not know anything about the 70s but it was not a problem as it turned out as most of them were quite happy chatting away by themselfs and they did not even need you to say is that right or wow or anything.

Their was 1 old man who did actually talk abt football Joe and his name was Willie I think and when he saw my tracksuit he said oh you are a footballer eh and I said yes I play for and he said I used to be a footballer as well until I got enjured playing for Aston Villa and he started going on and on abt Aston Villa and of coarse Joe it did not seem very likely to me that a wee old guy in a dressing gown used to play for Aston Villa and I thought he might be a bit confused but it was hard to tell and so I listened to him talk abt what a great player he had been until it started to get me down a bit Joe as I kept thinking that maybe 1 day I will be in that same bed in that same hospital and when I talk abt everything I achieved in football there will maybe be someone there who doesent believe me and thinks I have lost my marbles and of coarse I will have no way of proveing it and it makes you think Joe that everything you do might be for nothing in the end and no one will even know if you did it or not so what is the point.

Well after that Joe I was ready to check in to the hospital myself and get it over with so to speak but we still had to go down to the pediatric ward 1$^{st}$ and the woman who was maybe a nurse said that they had all kinds of young people their and when you see a childrens hospital on the tv or something Joe it is always reely bright colours and lots of toys and all the children are smileing and being brave but it is not like that in real life Joe and you can see everything needs a new coat of paint and the toys are the same age as we are and the kids are not having fun at all and why woud they Joe when they are not well and when I saw them their all lying in their beds I thought abt not even getting out of the elevator but I guessed I had to. We split up into 2 pairs and I went around the beds with Brady saying hello and talking to the kids and you dont ask them what it is wrong with them or anything Joe but most of them wind up telling you and it woud brake your heart to here some of there storys Joe and with the old folk I was on my guard on acct I did not want to say or do anything that might make me look stupid but when we were speaking to the kids I felt like I woud have done anything to cheer them up Joe just because the whole thing is just so desprit.

We were there for almost 1 hour Joe and we got round just abt everybody and the last person we spoke to was a little boy who coud hardly speak but he got all exited when he saw us and he said that he used to play football before he got ill and I asked him if he wanted to be a professhunal footballer when he grew up and he said yes and I said well I hope you will come and play for us and he said no he wanted to play for a big team and I said well we woud be a big team you were playing for us and he said ok he woud think abt it.

Well after that the woman who was maybe a nurse told us that the kids were a bit tired out now and we woud have to finish there and we said goodbye and got our photos taken and Brady talked all the way home abt nothing in particular and I woud not exactly say I had a grate night after that Joe but at lease I felt like I had done something useful and it had not been a wasted day and you can play all the football in the world Joe but it will not mean anything at the end of the day if you did not do some good from time to time.

Your pal,

Andy

May 4th

Well Joe that draw on Satterday means we are finely
safe from relegation for another year and there was big
celebrations in the changeing room which is to say we
got ¼ of a plastic cup of battery acid each and a speech
from old Donaldson abt how we shoud not let our
standards slip and we have to keep fighting to pick up
the points and finish as high up the table as we can and
I have got to say Joe that altho old Donaldson does not
know anything abt football or strategy he is a kind of
world authority on raining on peoples parades and sints
nobody at the club was planning on throwing the rest
of our games as soon as we were safe it was a bit of a
waste of his breath so to speak.

Of coarse what old Donaldson is reely getting at is
that we have 2 more league games to play and not just
the semi final and maybe the final of the cup altho that
is what the players are manely talking abt. I did not
think it was possible to be as old as Brady and never
have made it to a cup final but apparently it is and in

fact none of us have ever played in a final sints we were at primary school and even old Vidian says he has never played in 1 altho it is hard to tell if he understands what you are on abt or is even listening sometimes and I guess if I spoke another language I woud not make too much effort to learn English if it meant listening to Drummond talking abt a film he just saw that sounds like it might be Avatar only lots of bits sound quite diffrent so you do not know for sure that it is.

Everybody is beside themselves abt this semi final on Satterday Joe and I guess I am a bit exited for it myself altho of coarse I am not worried abt it being my last chance to play in a final Joe as I will be using winners medals for keyrings by the time I hang up my boots. But it will be a chance to make a little bit of club history I guess as the club has not been in a cup final sints 1974 or something so if Brady has never played in a final he must of been visiting the grandkids that weekend.

I guess what old Donaldson is getting at Joe is that we shoud not build up our hopes too much as everyone is talking as if we are already in the final and we have still got to beat Falkirk on Satterday at Hampden first. There is no films abt a plucky team of underdogs that gets to the semi final of a big competition and then gets put out by a team from the league below them Joe so nobody thinks it can happen to us but of coarse Joe it is a cup tie and in the last round old Donaldson put me on from the start so it just goes to show you that anything is possible.

So everyone is kind of running around in a flap and nobody is thinking past this semi final and I am keeping my cards close to my chest abt it Joe but if I get on against Falkirk on Satterday I will only have to play 2 more games to get my contract extension so if I can keep clear of trouble for 15 minutes or so on Satterday I will be home and hosed as they say. I do not want to jinks it so I have not mentioned it to anyone but I have played the right number of games and even the match programs say so and I called old Harry to check it out with him and at first he said he hadent heard of that kind of deal before but then he went and looked it up on the Internet and said yes apparently it happens all the time in football tho of coarse he woud want to negotiate the terms of my new contract so that I was getting quite a bit more money and that way we will both come out ahead.

So between you and me Joe I am kind of hoping the game is prity much over by the time I get on as the last thing I need when I am so close to that extension is a task force of confirmed maniacs from the next league down trying to break my leg off at the thigh for 15 minutes and in a way Joe I will not even be that disapointed if I do not get on as our next league game is against Motherwell and no offense to them Joe but their hardest player goes off when the mascots leave the field.

We each got 2 free tickets to the game Joe but I did not think you woud want to come all the way here when you do not know if I am going to get on or not so I sold them to 1 of the other lads for £40 and I thought you woud prefer that as it means I am £40 closer to paying you back and of coarse I cannot give you the money right now on acct I need it for my phone bill but if I did not have the money for the phone bill I woud probily have needed to borrow it from you so you can see Joe that it is the same as if I had payed you the £40 back and the only diffrents is that I did not borrow it from you 1$^{st}$ so reely it is saveing time for both of us. I guess that might be quite hard for you to understand Joe but I have done the math and that is definitely how it works out.

Your pal,

Andy


May 10th


Well old Donaldson got his hooks into me this am Joe and he started off telling me how well I was doing in training and how hard I was working to take everything on board and by the end he had built things up to the point where I thought he was going to tell me I had been made king of the universe and so when he said that I woud be starting against Falkirk in the semi final I dident say anything for a minute on acct that I thought he was going to keep on talking and tell me what my real reward was.

Well I tried to act all greatful and suprised abt it Joe on acct there is no point hurting an old mans feelings for no good reason but for 1 thing Joe the clubs whole season is resting on this 1 game so it is not exactly a huge sacrifice for Donaldson to finely play his best midfeilder and for another thing Joe the last thing I need right now is to spend 90 minutes within stabbing distance of a crack squad of brickies and lorry drivers who have just been told this is the biggest game of there lifes. But of coarse there is nothing I can say abt it Joe and however much sense it might make to me and you there is no way of explaneing it to anyone else that they woud understand and I have already herd abt 1000000 people telling me how they woud give there right arm to play in a cup final and of coarse Joe for them it is just a figure of speech but for me it is an actual real choice and these are guys who will kill a man as soon as look at him and woud torch our entire stadium with us in it for a fiver and a pack of regal king size. There is a reason they call them giant killers Joe and it seems to me like the little teams shoud have their own seperate cup that can be like the Hunger Games or whatever as it is not no odds if someone brakes their leg during a Forfar v Alloa game sints players at that level are 10 a penny and you coud go down the job centre and get another ½ a dozen that are just as good but if someone brakes my leg Joe that coud set Scottish football back 20 years and I dont mean to big myself up Joe but there is a reason I am not playing for Alloa and it is not just to do with not knowing where it is.

Well Joe as I say there is no getting out of it and I will just have to take it on the chin and hopefully that is the only place I take 1 tomorrow as it will be a free for all and reely they shoud have a guest referee for these games like they do in wrestling and if it was the ED209 robot from Robocop that was in charge tomorrow I still woud not get a wink of sleep for thinking abt it. But I guess it is not everybody that gets to play the final match of their career at Hampden and I hear the medical facilitys there are second to none so I supose that is something to look forward to at lease.

Your pal,

Andy


May 12th


Well Joe it all came off exactly as we planned and we just went out their and stuck to our game plan and it dident matter that our game plan was an utter shambels as their boys dident look like they had set eyes on each other before today and I guess the real Falkirk team must be tied up in a cupboard somewhere Joe because today was like taking candy from a baby. Old Donaldson made sure he was front and center as usual Joe and the reporters were falling all over themselfs to say what a master stroke it was to save me for this game and wrap me up in cotton wool so to speak but I guess none of them have dropped by our training ground recently as if they supose Donaldson has been wrapping me up in cotton wool recently they woud probily think Guatanamo Bay is a country club for retired terrorists.

But what I am getting at Joe is that Falkirk had no

answers yesterday and I shoud not have worried abt getting enjured as they did not get near enough to lay a finger on me and they spent so much time scrapping with Brady that they forgot all abt me. Well Joe you can bet that I remembered them I was there and they was 2 goals down before they put a man on me but they might as well have put an Elastoplast on a bullet hole for all the good it did and by half time we were 3 goals up and that was game over.

The last ½ hour was kind of a party Joe and I was worried that if the game got beyond Falkirks reach they woud sort of turn savage and start trying to get their lb of flesh but once the 3$^{rd}$ goal went in they just gave up Joe and they had that empty look on their face that people get when they are watching their train pull away from the platform and if it was a fight Joe you woud have stopped it their and then. But of coarse Joe that is not how football works and we did not score on them again but we just sort of kept the ball and played defence but even at that Joe old Brady was not satisfied and was giving us both barels whenever we did something that was not good enough to hang in a gallery and when Falkirk accidentally got a corner with 2 minutes left he balled me out for not picking up my man and I supose Brady thinks Maradona coud have been a grate player if he had just been a bit stronger in the tackle. But the proof of the pudding is in the eating Joe and it was not old Brady who got the sponsors man of the match award so I guess they must not have herd all the quality moaning that he was doing and thought that I was playing well off my own back and not because Brady was telling me to.

But anyway Joe that is us threw to the final and everyone wants to talk to me all over again tho of coarse it will all be abt what a tactical genius old Donaldson is as if it was down to him that Falkirk cant string a pass together and putting me on took abt as much genius as pulling a gun in a knifefight. But that is the way it goes Joe and if we actually win the cup I guess they will just give all the medals to old Donaldson and they wont even have to splash out for an open top bus as 1 of the charemen will just tow him around town on a skateboard.

Your pal,

Andy


May 14th


Well Joe you woud think after Satterday people woud be cueing around the block to shake my hand and thank me for getting them to a final but 2 days is a long time in football Joe and it is another 2 weeks until the final and nobody wants to give me too much credit in case I get their place in the team and they wind up watching on tv. Altho I do not know what makes them think it is their place in the team Joe as possession is 9/10ths of the law and the last time I checked the 1$^{st}$ choice midfeild at this club was Fairbairn and Brady and so really they shoud be trying to prove theirselfs against me or rather Brady and not the other way around.

So when old Donaldson called me in to his office this am Joe I knew enough not to expect a round of applause but I did not expect him to be sitting their with the chareman staring at me as if I had just punched a swan. He has got a funny sents of humour Joe and I thought maybe he was just pranking me and so all the wile he was shaking his head and talking abt how much the club have done for me I was waiting for him to bust out laughing and offer me a new contract and then all of a sudden the chareman asked me where I got the boots I was wearing on Satterday.

Well Joe they were 1 of the pairs Harry got me and when I said that the chareman shot forward in his seat and said and who the hell is Harry when he is at home. So I told them Harry was my agent and the chareman looked at me as if I had announced he was my partner at the beanbag factory and he said well is their a phone number for the bar he is propping up right now and old Donaldson chimed in and said sints when do you have an agent. Well I told them how Harry had got in their 1st after my goal in the darby and the chareman groned and threw up his hands and old Donaldson rubbed his face and said well Andy for 1 thing you are suposed to let the club know when you sign with an agent and for another thing the club has already got a sponsorship deal for its youth players and any agent worth his salt woud know that. As it is you and your wee pal have cost this club quite a bit of money and I only hope you have not given him any cash of your own as the club can just abt afford it but you cant.

Well Joe I do not see where old Donaldson gets off putting his nose into my finances never mind anything else and I was wondring whether to say that when the chareman bust in and said now you listen here son I do not care a good goddamn whether you have handed this shyster the keys to your house all I am concerned abt is the good of this club and you have given us a real headache here with this nonsents and frankly if it was up to me I woud have you clearing your locker for breach of contract and see how keen your agent was to represent you when he was earning 10% of 0 but of coarse I just sign the checks around here and Barry has persuaded me that you do not know what you are doing and I guess it does not take no Clarence Darrow to make that case but I will tell you this son this club has bent over backwards for you and you had better sharpen up prity fast because the next mistake you make will be on your own dime you understand.

Well to be honest Joe I did not totally understand but I guess I got the gist of it and I woud have stood and popped him 1 on the jaw if old Donaldson had not jumped in at that point and said everybody makes stupid mistakes when they are young and this is a real doozy you have pulled Andy but at lease we have caught it before it got out of hand and the club will deal with the sponsorship side of things but what you will need to do is go and explane to your pal Harry that he is not your agent no more and if the time ever comes where it is worth your wile to sign up with an agent the club will give you advice on that but for now you do not need a football agent no more than my auntie Aggie does and maybe even a bit less right now.

Well Joe I coud not reely say anything to that and when I texted Harry he coud not be my agent no more he was frantick and he phoned me up and asked me what I meant and I told him what the club had said abt how I was not aloud to have him as my agent any more and I thought he was going to bust out crying Joe and he kept asking to be aloud to speak to the manager and asking what the managers name was and finely he went quiet and said ok fine but I will need all those boots back as my mate will want them for someone else and I asked him what he meant and it turned out that the sponsorship deal he had got me was not with Nike but with his friend who is assistant manager at Sports Direct and had some old stock he coudent sell and had come up with sponsorship as a way of getting rid of it.

Well Joe it is all over now and I guess it tells you a lot abt the kind of deal the club have got us roped in to that some knock off boots from Sports Direct were better than the ones I was already wearing but there is no point crying over spoilt milk as otherwise you just wind up like our chareman going on and on abt stuff that happened in the past and is just ancient history now. I do not see where him or Donaldson get off telling me if I am aloud to have an agent or not never mind who says they are aloud to choose my agent for me and if that was the case the club coud offer me anything they liked and the agent they chose woud just agree to it and they woud be laughing all the way to the bank and me left holding the bill but I guess I am a bit smarter than they think Joe and they will see that soon enough.

Your pal,

Andy


May 17th


Well Joe now that the league is prity much over even old Donaldson cannot think of no alibi to keep me out of the team and he will have an even harder time now sints I gave old Ross Country the run around. I guess you will have seen what kind of show I put on for them Joe and my $2^{nd}$ goal was a peach altho anyone with a football brane will know that it was the $1^{st}$ goal that was the real vintage as anybody can hit a 30yd raker if you give them enough oppertunitys but it takes vision to see the keeper off his line like that. That is something they just cannot teach you Joe no matter how much time you spend practising free kicks with your dad.

So that is 2 man of the match awards out of 2 for me Joe and we will get a big send off from our fans in our last home game against Dundee. I coud reely do with the win bonus for that 1 even tho the game is not important and all anyone is worried abt is not getting enjured before the final. The alibis is going in nice and early Joe and there is hardly a player on 2 legs that is not suddenly going abt with a knee brace on 1 of them and of coarse I woud probily rather sit the game out myself but I have got to make this 1 last appearance that I need for my extension and that way I will have got the monkey off my back so to speak and I can go in to the final with my head clear and my mind focused on victory plus the win bonus against Dundee is £500 pounds Joe even though the game means exactly 0 so it woud be crazy to pass up on a loophole like that. I only wish all these newspaper men were so keen to splash the cash and when I met that guy from the Daily Record at Costa today you woud have thought that instead of the check sitting on the table it was a revolver with 1 bullet left in it.

Your pal,

Andy


May 20th


Well Joe that is me done with the media bit and after you have been threw it once before it is reely just more of the same. You woud think a lot of stuff to do with football woud be prity much common knowledge by now but it seems like it is not and all anybody can ever think to ask you is what it feels like to score a big goal in such a big game. Well it does not realy feel like anything Joe if I am honest with you and in some ways it is kind of like Xmas Day when you are building up to it for months and then 2 minutes later you are standing in all this junk and wondring what the fuss was all abt.

Well I did not say that to any of the reporters Joe as their eyes glaze over after abt 8 seconds and with the last lot I tried to say something intresting abt modern football but they just left all that out and kept in the bits abt how much I love scoring goals so it is pointless trying to explane it to them and I guess I will just save the juicy stuff for who ever writes my autobiography.

The other thing that sort of bugs me Joe is the reporters have always got to come up with some kind of angle to make it intresting and last time it was the rags to riches thing abt me coming from Selkirk and this time it is the rags to riches thing abt me coming from Selkirk. Only it is starting to get a bit old now Joe so whenever the reporters started poking around for storys abt how bad things were at Selkirk FC I just told them that their was not such a big diffrents between the premier league and Selkirk as they might think and in fact the mane diffrents was that at Selkirk I got to play football every once in a wile.

When you get famous Joe you sort of think people will be intrested in what you have to say and maybe they woud be if the reporters dident always twist it to make it sound diffrent than it is and I told them all abt my busness qualifications and the things I woud change around the club if I was in charge and you woud think that woud be more intresting than what it is like to score a goal but of coarse it wont be Joe and when the articles come out tomorrow they will all be abt how great it was to play at Hampden only 1 year after turning out at places like Hawick and Innerleith etc. Well I dont see what is so bad abt Innerleith Joe and all that is really holding it back is the mess but I guess moneing abt dog muck does not sell no newspapers or else wee Sandy at the Border Telegraph woud be a multimillionaire.

Your pal,

Andy


May 22nd


So I got in to training this am Joe and the 1$^{st}$ thing that happen was old Donaldson pulled me in to his office and said well Andy I have done my best to protect you from yourself but this time you have gone too far and there is nothing I can say to the chareman that is going to change that.

Well Joe I just thought it was another 1 of Bradys practical jokes and I said what do you mean and Donaldson picked up a newspaper off the desk and turned to the back pages and started reading. It was 1 of the interviews I did a few days ago and they had got what I said back to front as what I was trying to say was that Selkirk FC was a prity good club and I had a nice time their but they had twisted it all around so that it sounded like I was putting the boot in to my own club and saying how unproffeshunal they are and how bad our training is and how unhappy I am abt not getting to play every week and I guess I might have said something a bit like that Joe but not in those exact words.

Well Joe old Donaldson put down that newspaper and picked up another and then another and prity much all of them had the same bits slagging off the club and the manager and the other players and of coarse Joe some of it was meant tongue in cheek but that does not realy come across in a newspaper and I guess it sounded prity bad but then if you read in a newspaper that I was slagging you off Joe you woud not fly off the handle and you woud trust that I was only jokeing or that the reporter had got the wrong end of the stick and I tried to say that to old Donaldson but he cut me off and said yes I am sure it is an honest mistake and that is the problem Andy you are too honest for your own good. I have just had the chareman on the phone and he has told me that you will be training with the youth team from now on and I had to agree with him Andy as you have upset too many people around the club for me to keep you in the 1$^{st}$ team now.

Well Joe I did not say anything and old Donaldson sat back down and said the youth team are not training today so you can just clear out your locker and go home for the rest of today and then he started writeing on something and I guess that was him telling me it was over and their was no point saying anything.

I went into the changing room to get my stuff Joe and a few of the lads were their already but they went quiet soon as I went in and none of them looked at me or said anything not even Brady so I just came home and that is where I am now and I am watching shinty on the tv Joe and thinking abt that 1 appearance I need to make for my extension and wondring what I am the hell I am suposed to do. I guess old Donaldson wants me to appologise and I am man enough to hold my hands up and admit that the reporters got it wrong but he made it sound like every single person at the club is mad at me and I do not mind saying sorry to a couple of people Joe or to everybody all at once if someone got them all together but I am not going up to each separate dinner lady on bended knee and if anything Joe they shoud be appologising to me for all the comments and the eye rolling over the last few months. Well if I am big enough to let bygons be bygons maybe they shoud be too and if they are waiting for me to say sorry to the security guy with the combover Joe they are in for a long wait.

Your pal,

Andy

May 25th

Well Joe I guess when old Donaldson says something he means it exept when it is to do with contract extensions or giveing someone a chance in the 1ˢᵗ team and this time he has been as good as his word and I have been sent down to the youths. The youth team has finished there season already and everybody has been told if they are being kept on so you coud not even call it going threw the motions Joe as half of them know that they are safe for another year and the other half are ringing round everyone they know to see if they can get a deal or a trial or even just get put on the waiting list for a trial. It is reely depressing to watch the hope draining away from them all Joe and when 1 of them comes into the changing room and says he has managed to get a trial with Albion Rovers and everyone else perks up a little as if to say well it shows you that there is hope yet it just makes you want to shoot yourself.

I guess the work load here is not heavy Joe and at lease 1 person has come out of the deal happy sints they have promoted Burdon back up to the 1ˢᵗ team in my place. I bumped in to him at the changing room door just as he was comeing out which I guess is what you call irony Joe and he gave me his big cheesy grin but it did not bother me none Joe as he had a big armful of stuff he was moveing out of his locker and into his new 1 and there is only so seriesly you can take anyone when they are carrying talcum powder and sensitive skin body wash.

Well it has been nearly a week now Joe and if old Donaldson is not careful he is going to wind up letting my contract run out without tieing me down to a new 1 and the next time he asks me to come into his office will be the last time as I will be off to another club so fast his head will spin. I kind of wish I had not given old Harry the elbow now Joe as it woud have been handy to have someone going around getting my name out their to other clubs and you cannot reely do that stuff yourself Joe as you are libel to look like a desprit no hoper and that is not reely the way forward for me right now. Of coarse it woud be handy if 1 of the newspapers did an article on me and how I am abt to become a free agent in the summer and sints it is thanks to them that I am in this mess you woud think that was the lease they coud do but nobody is intrested Joe not even on the club forums and I have tried getting a little bit of debate going on the boards but most people just say it is quite right I shoud go down to the youths for a bit after what I said and that I will lern a lesson from it but of coarse Joe they do not know that I am on the verge of walking away from the club scot free and if they did it woud be a diffrent story all together but I cannot tell them that Joe as it woud look a bit fishy if someone went on the boards who knew all the inns and outs of my contract and even the reely stupid ones woud be libel to put 2 + 2 together if I did that and these are people who think that wrestling is real Joe so we are not exactly talking branes of Britain here.

So I guess I am kind of caught between a rock and a hard place for now Joe and there is only 1 league game plus the cup final to go so if the club want to nail me down to another contract they will have to bring me back up to the 1st team this week reely and if they do not it will be time for me to start scouting out the horizon so to speak. Of coarse it will probily not come to that Joe as this is a club which has got CCTV in the toilets to stop you stealing toilet roll and they are not abt to let a multi million £ asset like myself walk away for free but if it looks like they might then it woud help me out a lot Joe if you pretended to be my agent and maybe phoned around a few clubs to sort of gage the intrest levels and get a bidding war going and of coarse I woud not give you 10% of my salary Joe as it woud only be for pretend but it woud be the quickest way to get your money back and especially if I got a club who were willing to pay me a signing on bonus and reely that woud be ideal Joe but I will give you the nod on that when I am ready and you shoud probily not do anything just yet until I let you know as old Donaldson has eyes and spies everywhere Joe and I can hardly change channels on my tv without him calling me up and asking me what is wrong with the horse racing. In the meantime Joe you coud maybe start trying to make contacts at some other clubs as I do not reely know anyone anywhere else and when you send an email to the address on their websites they never answer you.

Well Joe like I say it probily wont come to that but if it does I guess it will be kind of exiting like back in the old days when you were my wingman and you woud always do what you coud to help out your old pal Andy and of coarse I woud do whatever I coud for you but that was not much as you were not ambitious like me and there is not much you can do to help someone out when all they want is a CSI marathon and a pudding supper from Haddies. But if you do me this favour Joe I will be sure to pay you back in kind only it woud not be by getting you a trial at a football club obviously as it woud need to be something realistic.

Your pal,

Andy


May 27th


Well Joe I guess you were only trying to help and of coarse I am greatful but for 1 thing I asked you to hang fire on asking around until I was sure I was not getting my contract extension and for another thing if you had thought abt it for even 1 second you woud of seen there is no point in me going on trial at Selkirk FC and it does not make any sents that I woud. I need a club that is going to pay me actual money Joe not just give me a 10% discount at the managers carpet shop and even if I was intrested in going back to Selkirk I woud not be going on trial their no more than I woud go for a  job interview at a charity shop. I do not know where your head is at these days Joe and I know that you mean well but stuff like this is reely exaspirating when I have already got enough on my plate to worry abt and a lot of people woud reely fly off the handle abt this Joe but it is just as well I have got the patients of a Saint as otherwise I do not know where I woud start.

The other thing is Joe that if you were going to ask around to see if there is any interest I wish that you had done it properly and the reason I know that you did not do it properly is that you did not get the right response and it is all very well for you to say that they have heard all abt me and do not want to get involved Joe but it is your job as my agent to get them intrested and to explane why they shoud sign me. That is busness 101 as they say Joe and if you have got a premier league footballer on your hands and the best you can do is get him a trial at Selkirk FC it is no wonder that the Tesco you work in is going bust as it is all abt presentation and being suttle and going abt things in a diffrent way eg telling the clubs that I am in huge demand and that they shoud move fast and not telling them that I am desprit and in debt and willing to listen to any offers. A 4 yr old coud see why that woud not work Joe and I am only telling you for your own good Joe as this is no way for a groan man to carry on.

But I supose you are only partly to blame Joe sints it is not reely your fault that I am in this mess in the 1$^{st}$ place and I shoud not loose the rag with you when you have always done your best by me up until today and I guess it shows you how desprit I am that I even asked you when I know that if I sent you to the shops for a packet of Quavers you woud come back with cheesy Wotsits. I am not having a go at you Joe and I am reely having a go at myself sints it is just in your nature to get things wrong and I shoud know by now that is never going to change.

Sints we are being honest Joe I probily woud have

told you to ring round the other clubs by now anyway as that is 2 weeks that I have been in the dog house and we have run out of games exept the cup final so I guess there is no chance old Donaldson is going to put me back into the team for that and even if he did it woud just show that he had been playing mind games all along and it is 1 thing to have someone sweating on their place in the team for a little bit but it is something else to have them worrying abt their actual future Joe and that is not the kind of manager I woud want to play for not for any amount of money.

Well I guess I will phone around the clubs myself Joe and I will have to pretend to be someone else as it is against the law to speak to other teams wile you are still under contract but then what is old Donaldson is going to do abt it as he has already sent me to the reserves and let my contract run down so unless he pulls out a gun and shoots me he is out of options and even if he did shoot me Joe he woud probily be doing me a favour. Maybe I will feel diffrently abt it when I have spoken to some other clubs Joe and I supose they will be lineing up around the block to talk to me and I woud even be willing to drop down a division or maybe 2 if the price was right. I do not know where I am placed on the wage scale Joe but even the guys from Falkirk did not have their watches held together with cellotape so it shows you that people in the lower leagues are on as much money as I am and it is just as well that I cannot drive Joe as even the kitchen ladys woud be laughing at my car if I could afford 1.

Well Joe thanks again for trying even though it was kind of a waste of everyones time and I hope you will read these emails properly next time as otherwise it is sort of pointless to keep writing them to you.

Your pal,

Andy


May 28th


Well Joe I called around pretending to be Harry and I guess you were right abt the other clubs altho it coudent have helped you going around scaring them off like you did but the fact is I rang abt 2 dozen diffrent clubs and I even tried Berwick Rangers Joe but I got nowhere and the guy who answers the phones at Annan Atletic said they might be interested in having a look at me later in the summer but later in the summer is no good to me Joe as I need money now and I looked up what the Annan players are on in Football Manager and I thought it must be their monthly wage instead of their weekly as there is no chance a normal human being coud get by on that.

I did some research on the Internet Joe and it turns out most clubs in Scotland are part time even the ones that are in proper leagues and most of their players have to get another job in order to support themselves which is ok for them but I have never had to work in a normal job before and I have got even less idea how to get 1 than I do abt finding a new club. I guess you are suposed to look in the job adverts in the paper and fill out an application form Joe but I never saw anybody in Selkirk do that and everyone I knew who had a job got it because their dad run the shop or something but my dad does not run a shop or anything else Joe so that is no good to me. I supose some people are able to get by on next to 0 money because they live with their parents but that is no help as I woud need to get my parents to move to Glasgow or Annan or wherever it is I wind up and it is hard enough getting my dad up out of bed in the am never mind halfway across the country.

Well I checked with the bank abt being aloud to miss my morgage payments for a little wile Joe until I get back on track but it seems that is not how it works and so I asked abt selling the flat back to them only they said they never sold me the flat in the 1$^{st}$ place just loned me the money to buy it from someone else so you can see Joe that they are desprit to get themselfs off the hook. They said I am aloud to sell the flat to someone else if I do not want it anymore but I will not get the money back as apparently I still owe it to the bank and in fact they told me that I probily woud wind up oweing them even more money if I sold the flat so what do you think abt that Joe and I bet it makes you think you are in the wrong game with the shelf stacking. Of coarse I have got a busness qualification and the whole point of that was so that I understood how busness works but the only problem with that Joe is that I only understand how busness is meant to work not how it actually does in reel life and you can know all the spreadsheets and memos in the world Joe but if someone gives you 50 thousand pounds to buy a house and then you sell the house for 50 thousand pounds and then the 1st people say that you still owe them money then it is easy to see that the game is rigged to stop ordnary people coming out ahead and I guess that is the one thing they do not teach you at busness school Joe as otherwise you woud just get depressed and give up the ghost and then where woud they find there next sucker.

We have always lived very diffrent lifes from each other Joe and I have always stuck up for you when anyone who tried to run you down but even I never thought I woud see the day when I woud swap places with you and maybe it is not quite as bad as all that old pal but it is certainly getting their. I guess with my busness qualification and your dads help I woud be able to get a job in Selkirk and I woud not mind staying at home with my folks if they coud just stop the dogs from going off there heads in the am and I am sure that my dad does it on purpose just to get me up but there is no need as no one coud sleep on that old mattress even for a bet. But the point is Joe there are worst things in the world than to have a happy life and these are suposed to be the best years of mine and I have spent this last 1 watching other people play football and getting buried under a pile of debt and you have not really writ to tell me how you are getting on Joe but I supose that is because you were too busy having a nice time and why shoudent you after all.

So I guess what I am saying is Joe that if you do not mind getting back on the phone and getting me that trial with Selkirk FC I woud appresiate it. I coud just as easy do it myself but I guess Selkirk have not signed many premier division footballers before and if anyone is going to be the 1st to make it happen it might as well be my old pal Joe who has always done right by me and never tried to make a penny out of it.

My contract runs until the week after the cup final so I might as well milk these last few days for every penny. I am getting free tickets to the final and it is the closest I will ever get to playing in 1 now so I will probily go along. I guess I coud try and sell the tickets Joe but I have been here 1 year and not made any friends so I woud not even know who to sell them to or for how much.

Well Joe I guess it is time I hit the old dusty trial. I will see you in the summer and maybe we will finely make that big trip to Miyorka that we always planned.

Your pal,

Andy

# Time Added On

May 29th

Well Joe they say you do not know what you have got until you have lost it and never were truer words spoken old pal and if there is a moral to this past year I woud say that is it. At school they can teach you everything they want abt busness or busness studies but at the end of the day everyone is diffrent and wants diffrent things and ½ the time they do not know themselfs how well they are doing or what they want out of life so how the hell can anybody else know. What I am saying Joe is you have got to choose your own path in life and stick to it no matter what anybody else says even if they think it looks reely depressing and pointless because for all they know that is maybe what you like abt it.

Anyway Joe I was not going to let what has happent put me off going to the final as nobody coud say I hadent earned it. I have not got any money anyway so if it had been free tickets to the bingo I woud probily have went just to get out of this house which is leeching me for every brass penny I got. I guess if a man has a wife and kids he can at lease say all his money is going to another human being but with me all my cash is dissapearing up the spout for the sake of a concrete wall that does not care if I live or die and every time I lie on the couch I wind up getting really angry abt how much money the sealing is costing me just by being there and that is no good Joe.

So I went in to the city centre in the am Joe just to kind of take in the cup final atmosphere but of coarse Joe their was 0 of that as the cup final atmosphere just means lots of people in pubs watching the early kick offs on tv and getting so drunk they will be ½ asleep by the time the final comes on. Their were a few scarfs going around here and their and I thought maybe someone might recognise me Joe but nobody did so I went into McDonalds for a strawberry milkshake as I guessed their was no point worrying abt loosing weight now that I am getting the big heave ho. Well Joe I was sitting their drinking my milkshake and kind of regretting not going the whole hog as they say and just buying everything I liked and the good thing abt

McDonalds Joe is that it is so cheap that even people with 0 money can come in and treat it like an all you can eat buffet. I guess that is why all the homeless people are always camped out outside Joe and when I watched 1 of them wolfing into a cheeseburger it seemed kind of funny somehow that on the day his team was playing their 1$^{st}$ cup final in 30 years a professhunal footballer was sitting in McDonalds feeling jealous of a tramp.

So I was up standing in the cue again Joe and it was so busy I coudent hear my phone ringing at 1st and when I finely answered it was old Jimmy the assistant manager asking me where I was. Well I was abt to tell a lie like I usually do Joe but I guessed their was no point and so I told him I was in McDonalds and he said yes you woud be a hard man to track down if they ever closed the food court at the st enochs centre and I started to tell him it was not that McDonalds I was at Joe but he just kept going. He said that they had only found out this am that Burdon was cup tied on acct he had already played in the cup this season and so they had no other registered midfeilders and they needed me at Hampden right away. And I said okay I will be their in 2 hours and he said what are you talking abt and I said well it is a 2 hours walk and he said what the hell McDonalds are you at son the Timbucktoo branch and I started to tell him which McDonalds I was at again Joe but he cut me off and said just get in a taxi Andy and the club will pay for it.

Well Joe when the taxi pooled up at Hampden Joe old Jimmy was waiting outside for me and if you guessed he woud be pleased to see me you lost your bet as he stared at me like I had just staggered into the cafe he works at 2 minutes before it closes. But he got me in via the fire exit and took me into the dressing room and nobody there said anything to me either not Brady or Donaldson or nobody and if it had not been for my name on the teamsheet I woud of started to think I was a mirage. Even during the warm up nobody spoke to me and they only passed when they had to and you can probily guess that it was not exactly a laugh riot Joe but I just keeped thinking abt my share of the cup money and how it woud run into the 1000s and that was worth putting up with anything for.

Well Joe Hampden kept on filling up and up and the air was so hot it was hard to breath and then finely we came out the tunnel and their was a massive roar and the match got under way. Of coarse it was no newsflash to find that I was not playing Joe but when the ref blew his whistle and Brady turned and played the ball back to Drummond and the whole ground shook with people stamping there feet it was the 1$^{st}$ time I had thought it shoud of been me out there taking that kick off instead of sitting up the back of the dugout with empty seats on either side of me. But then we went 1-0 down and after that people kind of forgot that they were suposed to hate me and they stopped making such a performance out of not speaking to me.

I guess you will not have been watching the game Joe as your old pal Andy was not going to be playing but the thing abt cup finals is the more keyed up the players are the worst the football is and when you are at home watching every pass come down with snow on it it is easy to believe you must be 1 of the top 10 footballers in the country but when you are actually their in the stadium Joe it is a totally diffrent situation and if someone is able to play there best football with a hundred 1000 people banking on there every move you can bet they are just 1 of those people who do not care about anything exept theirselfs and maybe not even that. So it was not much of a game Joe on acct everybody was so desprit to do their best and it was still 1-0 all the way into enjury time when Drummond pulled up with cramp and old Donaldson put his hands on his head and looked around at the bench. Well Joe his eyes went right past me 3 times but by then I was the only player he had left who was not a defender and I guess he did not think he had no other option because he pointed at me and beckoned me over and said to me get stripped son you are going on.

And it was strange Joe after 3 hours of the silent treatment to all of a sudden be bombarded with noise and I was up their standing on the touchline with Donaldson shouting on one side of me and Jimmy on the other and thousands of fans on the stairs and in the stands and all of them telling me what to do and after not having kicked a ball for weeks Joe I did not expect the next time I stepped on to a football pitch to be at

Hampden park with the announcer saying on comes number 28 Andy Fairbairn and everybody in the stadium going absolutely mental and even the rest of my team applauding and as I came on Brady grabbed me by the arm and said this is your chance son 1 goal here and all is forgiven. And so I ran up into the penalty box and waited for the corner kick to come in.

I guess old Brady must have known what I was going to try Joe sints I had already done it once before and when I peeled off he stepped right in their with the screen and suddenly I had a clear run on at the far post and I was in and jumping right up over there full back like he was a drystone dyke and I hung up there in the air and then the ball fell out of the floodlights and onto my head and flew into the stanchion and went out.

I watched the ball rolling along the running track Joe and even though I heard the whistle blow and half the stadium go crazy it seemed like someone should go and get it and I went and picked it up but by then the pitch was swarming and the only square inch of the stadium that dident have abt 1000 people in it was the bit where I was standing and I dident know where else to go so I just started walking around the running track with the ball in my hands.

Well by now the tannoy was playing We Are The Champions and everyone was singing and dancing and I supose I shoud of felt on top of the world myself Joe seeing as I had just made my contract extension and woudent be going back to Selkirk no more but I dident feel that way at all and I guess the ball must of rolled into a puddle before I picked it up Joe because their was rain all over my face and on my hands and on my sleeves where I had wiped it off and I do not know who makes our strips Joe but you woud be as well trying to mop up water with a crisp packet as with 1 of these shirts.

So when I got back to the dugout I wasent sure if the silent treatment woud cancel out the shouting at or the other way around and when Brady saw me I thought he was going to take a swing at me but he dident he just put his arm round me and said its ok wee man tomorow is another day and you will be back here before you know it and everybody else came round and patted me on the back and said the same thing exept from Vidian who was going around taking pictures with a big smile on his face and sometimes I wonder abt him if I am honest with you Joe.

So then we lined up to get our runners up medals Joe and I looked round at Brady and Drummond and even old Donaldson and they all looked so gutted and I guess Brady is right that I am still young and it is only right that I shoud get another shot at it but how is it right if only 1 person gets what is comeing to them Joe and even if I play every cup final from here until the end of time it woud not count for 0 if none of them ever got back here with me. A fare market has got to be fare to everyone Joe that is the only way it can work.

So coud you let the folk at Selkirk know I wont be needing that trial Joe as I will be staying here and getting this club back to where it belongs ie back to Hampden Park only this time it will be to win. I supose the chareman will say that I owe Selkirk a cup final as well and he will not be not wrong Joe but if he coud see old Brady trying to remember the password for his phone in the am he woud understand why time is running out and I have got to prioritise. I guess

Miyorka will have to wait Joe as I am going to have a lot going on but their is more to life than football as they say and however many cup finals in I am playing or how much money I am making I hope you know I wont forget my promise to my old pal Joe.

Your pal,

Andy

P.S. Joe I told everyone afterwards the drinks were on me only it works differently in real life than in films and if you could lone me another £100 Joe I woud reely appresiate it.

Printed in Great Britain
by Amazon